Merry Chri[illegible]
from
Mrs. Shipman

1998
1999

OLIVER TWIST

Retold by Linda Elliott Long

LANDOLL, INC.

Ashland, Ohio 44805

Contents

CHAPTER 1

Alone and Afraid

In an English town nearly two hundred years ago, a baby boy was born named Oliver Twist. He was born in a government workhouse: a place where poor people worked until they could pay their many over-due bills.

His beautiful, young mother, weak and pale after his delivery, said sadly to the workhouse doctor, "Let me hold him now, before I die."

She kissed Oliver's forehead, laid her poor head back on the humble cot and died.

Oliver and his mother were so very alone that neither family nor friends were present on this momentous day of life and death.

"Such a lovely, young mother—who was she, nurse?" the doctor asked.

"I don't know," answered the workhouse nurse. "Someone found her passed out in the street last night. She was dressed in rags, poor thing, and carried no identification."

"No, not even a wedding ring," the doctor said, as he looked at the young lady's delicate left hand. "Well, do what you can for the child," the doctor instructed the nurse before leaving. "You can feed him some gruel."

Gruel, a watery oatmeal-soup, and a tattered old blanket were the only provisions offered to Oliver Twist to welcome his birth. It is no wonder that the orphan cried and cried.

There was no where else for Oliver Twist to live, so he remained in the workhouse and was given very little care. It was a wonder that the baby even survived. In those days, the workhouses were run by supervisors who were in charge of several workhouses in the surrounding countryside. Housemothers looked after the juveniles who were jailed there because they had broken "poor" laws. The housemothers received small allowances of tax money to feed and clothe these "paupers," as they were called.

Baby Oliver's housemother, Mrs. Mann, was mean, selfish, and dishonest. Instead of using the allowance—small as it was—for the children's needs, she used most of the money for herself. Her care of the children was neither kind, nor generous, nor even safe.

Mrs. Mann was, however, skillful at hiding her rough treatment of the juveniles. Whenever an official checked her workhouse, Mrs. Mann made sure the children looked in good condition. That is, until the official, Mr. Bumble, wrote a good report and went on his way to visit the next workhouse.

Time passed. After nine years of little food and much sorrow, Oliver was physically frail but amazingly strong in spirit. Perhaps he inherited his soul-strength from his coura-

geous mother—Oliver certainly hoped that was so.

It was his soul-strength that helped him endure days like his ninth birthday, which he spent in a detention cell with two other workhouse paupers. Mrs. Mann chose this punishment for the three children because they had dared to tell her they were hungry!

On this very day, Mr. Bumble made a surprise visit to Mrs. Mann and the children in her care. He came with important business as, indeed, Mr. Bumble was convinced that everything he did was of the utmost importance! The government had a rule: when an orphan reached nine years of age, it was time for him to start earning a wage to pay his keep. Mr. Bumble had, therefore, come to take Oliver on his way to an even crueler chapter of his sad, young life.

CHAPTER 2

Not Welcome

Oliver hurried after Mr. Bumble as quickly as he could until they had completed their walk to the town workhouse. Soon after their arrival, Mr. Bumble told Oliver he was to appear before the "board" where he would receive his labor assignment.

Oliver followed Mr. Bumble into a large room, which he guessed must be the "board" room, where he saw ten stern-looking men sitting at a long table. Mr. Limbkins, who must have been the "head" of the board, snapped nastily to Oliver, "What's your name? And do you have a trade?"

Oliver shook with fear. He had never before been interrogated by so many stern faces.

Irritated by Oliver's nervous shaking, Mr. Bumble swatted Oliver's back with his cane.

Oliver had not expected the painful assault, so he began to cry. His voice cracked as he tried to answer. His choking seemed to amuse the ten pitiless gentlemen who laughed uproariously at Oliver Twist.

"We might expect such crude behavior from a pauper...from a drain on the taxes these past nine years," Mr. Limbkins remarked to the board.

"Yes, it is time he pays for his keep," they all sternly agreed.

"Oliver Twist," ordered the head board member, "tomorrow at 6 a.m. you will begin your first shift of picking oakum." Picking oakum was the tedious task of separating the threads of used rope to make single strands of insulating material to stick in the crevices of wooden boats.

Thus ended the board meeting, whereupon Mr. Bumble led Oliver to a large room where many hard cots were crammed uncomfortably together. Oliver lay on one of them and cried himself to sleep.

For the next six months, Oliver's regimen (and that of the several poor souls assigned to work duties) consisted of the following:

A work schedule lasting from sunrise to sundown.

A meal schedule of one bowl of watery gruel for breakfast, lunch, and supper, one onion twice a week, and one bread roll on Sundays.

The combination of long hours of exhausting work and insufficient nutrition made Oliver and the other boys crazy with hunger. They were slowly starving to death.

The boys decided that one of them must beg the kitchen master for more food. They drew straws to select the unlucky fellow who should make this humble request. Oliver Twist picked the shortest straw.

So, at supper that evening, after all the boys had scraped every last morsel of oatmeal from their bowls, each of them stared pleadingly at Oliver to see if he would keep the bargain.

His stomach aching with emptiness and fear, Oliver got up from the table, walked slowly to the kitchen master, and said, "Please, sir, may I have some more?"

The robust kitchen master nearly lost his voice in disbelief at Oliver's astonishing request.

"What?" his hoarse voice hissed at Oliver.

Oliver added bravely, "Please, sir, may we have some more?"

In angry reply, the master lifted the heavy serving spoon and whacked Oliver over the head again and again. Furiously, the kitchen master screamed for Mr. Bumble to remove Oliver immediately!

Mr. Bumble heard the commotion and pulled Oliver away from the swinging arms of the kitchen master. He marched the young orphan directly to Mr. Limbkins, who was meeting with the board that very evening in the chambers.

"Mr. Limbkins, sir," shouted Mr. Bumble, "this ungrateful child has asked for more!"

"What an incredible request!" one of the board members remarked. "The nerve of the child! His kind is no good. I predict he will be hanged some day."

Having no compassion and insensitive to the needs of others, the ten men replied in unison, "Send him to solitary confinement. Add his name to the list of those who may stay here no longer!"

The next morning, the name of Oliver Twist appeared on a poster outside the workhouse that read:

> "REWARD—five pounds sterling silver to anyone who will take one Oliver Twist from our premises."

Oliver was, in effect, offered "for sale" to anyone who needed an apprentice for a shop or business.

The workhouse officials kept Oliver confined for days. All day he cried, all night he slept fitfully—awaking in the darkness only to be reminded of his miserable loneliness. When he was allowed in the presence of the other boys, it was only so that they could see him beaten as a warning that no one else should follow Oliver's "bad" example of behavior.

A week passed, after which a chimney sweep named Mr. Gamfield happened to walk past the workhouse. His thoughts were a bit distracted by his many overdue bills, but not too distracted to notice the "Reward" sign posted for Oliver Twist. The sign interested Mr. Gamfield greatly, for five pounds sterling silver was exactly the amount he needed to pay the bill collector.

Since Mr. Gamfield knew the ill-treatment the workhouse children endured, he calculated it would cost him almost nothing to feed and clothe this young orphan. Five pounds sterling, free work from the boy—Mr. Gamfield figured he couldn't lose! Motivated by his own interests and giving no consideration to Oliver's welfare, Mr. Gamfield offered to make Oliver his apprentice in the dirty and dangerous trade of chimney sweeping.

The board discussed the proposal and noted the dangers of the trade, for it was well known that some children had suffocated from the chimney smoke while trying to clean

out the soot. However, the workhouse was losing money everyday that Oliver stayed there without earning a wage, so the board accepted the offer. A court appearance was arranged so that a judge could hear the case. He would sign a legal decree to transfer Oliver from the authority of the workhouse to the apprenticeship of Mr. Gamfield.

The next day, Mr. Bumble, Mr. Gamfield, and Oliver Twist stood before the judge awaiting

his decision. It was a tense moment for Oliver. One look at Mr. Gamfield's harsh face told Oliver that the man was not a person to trust.

To sway the judge to their side of the matter, Mr. Bumble lied by saying that Oliver had "always wanted to be a chimney sweep," and Mr. Gamfield lied by saying that "of course, he would take good care of the youngster."

Whereupon, the judge was just about to sign the decree when he noticed the expression of terror in Oliver Twist's face.

"What is it that is troubling you, child?" the judge asked.

Oliver knelt and humbly begged, "Please sir, do anything else, send me back to solitary confinement, anything. But please don't make me go with him. He frightens me."

Quickly, the judge tore up the decree and ordered Mr. Bumble to return him to the workhouse. And the next day, the "Reward" poster was nailed again upon the workhouse door.

CHAPTER 3

Nothing Good

A few days later, Mr. Sowerberry, the town undertaker, had an appointment at the workhouse with Mr. Bumble.

The two men began their business with a bit of small talk centering on the regretful fact of how hard it was for Mr. Sowerberry to earn much profit from coffin building.

During a lull in the conversation, Mr. Bumble's thoughts drifted to other subjects, and Oliver Twist came to his mind.

"Do you know anyone who can take an orphan-boy into his trade, Mr. Sowerberry? We have one here who has become rather a burden to us. We'll pay a reward."

"In that case, I can use the child myself," replied the undertaker.

Remembering the recent session before the judge, Mr. Bumble decided, however, not to bring this offer to court.

That evening, Oliver quietly followed Mr. Bumble through the dark streets to the undertaker's home.

Once inside the small parlor, lit dimly with candlelight, Mr. and Mrs. Sowerberry studied their new apprentice.

"A little fella, isn't he?" Mrs. Sowerberry seemed concerned over how much work this slight child could produce.

"Oh, he'll grow," Mr. Bumble quickly assured them.

"Yes, and it will be our groceries he'll grow on," complained the undertaker's wife. "He'll cost us much more than he's worth."

Her sour attitude was evident even more as she almost pushed Oliver downstairs towards a cold, damp cellar used as a pantry. A kitchen maid was sorting through some provisions just at that time.

"Charlotte," Mrs. Sowerberry called to the maid, "give the boy some of the supper scraps we had put out for the dog. Being a 'work-house pauper,' he'll be satisfied with whatever we give him to eat."

Indeed, Oliver ate every leftover scrap for he was very hungry. Then, Mrs. Sowerberry led him back upstairs to a room where empty coffins were stored. There was space in a corner for a small cot for Oliver, and this is where Oliver was to make his bed. The next morning, Oliver awoke to the sounds of someone kicking on the locked storeroom door.

"Let me in, I say," yelled a nasty voice.

Oliver moved the door chain slowly as the voice on the other side of the door screamed even louder, "You're a pauper from the work-house, aren't you?"

The mean voice continued, "The first thing I'm going to do is whoop you—so you'll know

I'm the head servant here. Now open this door before I kick it down."

Oliver bravely opened the door and peered up into the face of a young ruffian only a few years older than he, but much taller.

"My name is Noah Claypole, and I'm here to tell you that you'll be taking orders from me—is that clear?"

"Yes, sir." Oliver answered.

Noah was a "charity-boy," which meant his

parents were poor and he worked to help pay his keep. His classmates, who were more well-off than he, had teased Noah unmercifully for years about his lowly position in life. Noah believed that Oliver's arrival now gave him a big chance to feel superior to someone else, for an orphan-boy was looked down upon even more than a charity-boy.

For the next several weeks, Oliver endured the teasing of Noah and did his best to learn his assignments as the undertaker's newest apprentice.

Several days passed during which Mr. Sowerberry observed Oliver closely and noticed something about Oliver's facial expression that gave Mr. Sowerberry an idea. He spoke of it to his wife. "Have you noticed, my dear wife, what a deep look of despair is always on the face of young Oliver Twist?"

"He is a gloomy one," agreed the wife.

"He would make an excellent mute for our business!" the undertaker said with glee.

A mute was a person paid to be a silent mourner at a funeral or graveside service. It was all to the undertaker's advantage, of course, for if he could add the services of a mute to his funerals, he could charge his customers more money. It didn't matter that the mute had no true feelings for the dead person.

Mrs. Sowerberry agreed with her husband. At the next funeral, Mr. Sowerberry began teaching Oliver the trade of being a mute.

Oliver learned quickly, although it was a depressing business for a boy only ten years old. Mr. Sowerberry was pleased with his dramatic abilities. This caused Noah Claypole to become quite jealous of Oliver.

Noah's jealousy increased his ill-treatment of Oliver and prodded him to think of more devious ways to upset Oliver. For example, one day when Mr. Sowerberry was away, the ruffian sneered, "Tell me about your mother, Oliver."

"My mother died," Oliver said, "and I'd rather you say nothing about her."

"How did she die, little orphan?" Noah pressed.

"I think her heart was broken," Oliver said.

"I think she died because she was bad!" taunted Noah.

Stunned by the hurtful and uncalled for comment, Oliver grabbed Noah's throat in great anger. Mustering all his strength, Oliver punched the larger boy with such force that he knocked Noah flat on the floor!

"Help," screamed Noah. "Charlotte, help! He's killing me."

Charlotte, along with Mrs. Sowerberry, rushed to Noah's aid. Seeing Noah sprawled on the floor (although he could easily have arisen), both females started hitting and scratching the face and arms of small Oliver as if he were a dangerous threat to them.

Noah got up and joined them in the fight, whereupon Oliver's strength was quickly conquered. They pushed him down into a small fruit cellar and locked the door.

"What are we going to do?" lamented Mrs. Sowerberry. "Mr. Sowerberry's not here to protect us, and I'm sure that boy will knock down the cellar door in just a few minutes. I knew nothing good would come from a workhouse pauper!"

"Noah, get Mr. Bumble right away!" Mrs. Sowerberry screamed breathlessly.

Indeed, Mr. Bumble was called in, and Mr. Sowerberry soon returned home to find Mr.

Bumble, Mrs. Sowerberry, Noah, and Charlotte all frantically discussing the worthless deeds of the workhouse orphan who would surely come to no good. Mr. Sowerberry unlocked the cellar door and gave Oliver a painful thrashing for starting such a fight with Noah.

"Now, you've learned your lesson, have you, Oliver?" asked the undertaker smugly. "Whatever led you to react so violently?"

"He said bad things about my mother."

Mrs. Sowerberry, revealing her true sentiments about the poor boy, added, "Well, Noah is probably right!"

Oliver had as much of this topic as he could stand; and he cried, "You're lying!"

Shocked that an orphan-boy would speak back to her so ferociously, Mrs. Sowerberry, too, began to sniffle. Then, Mr. Sowerberry felt compelled to defend his wife's honor, so he thrashed Oliver again even harder than before and sent him to bed. There, Oliver dropped his tired, tortured body upon his cot and sobbed.

CHAPTER 4

Going to London

Darkness filled the room, and hours passed. Oliver looked around the dismal room, then out the window at the distant stars. They shone so brightly yet were so far away. *Could I ever get away?* he wondered. Somehow, he knew he must.

Oliver packed a few items of clothing, one hard biscuit he had saved from supper, and the one penny he had earned from Mr. Sowerberry. He ran away as soon as there was light in the eastern sky.

Oliver recollected the way Mr. Bumble had led him from the workhouse to the undertaker's home many months before. It was early in the morning when he passed the workhouse, and thinking everyone was still sleeping, Oliver peeked through a space in the outer fence to have one last look at the place of his birth.

To his surprise, there was someone up and weeding the garden: his little friend Dick who, even though a bit younger than Oliver, had withstood almost as many beatings and hunger pains as had Oliver.

Dick lifted his head and saw Oliver's face peering through the fence posts. The child ran to Oliver and stretched his arms through the rails almost to hug him if he could reach him.

"Shh!" Oliver cautioned. "Please don't let anyone know I'm running away."

Dick looked at Oliver with obedient eyes.

"It is so very good to see you, Dick, but you look so pale."

"The doctor said I am dying, but I am so thankful I saw you first, Oliver. Now, hurry, you must run before they find you."

"I will. But, Dick, I must believe I will see you again in happier times."

Oliver's little friend replied, "I know we will see each other in Heaven, if not before. God bless you, Oliver."

Dick's words touched Oliver greatly, for he had never received a blessing before. Then, Oliver continued on his way to London, a city he had heard was big enough to have plenty of jobs for a poor boy to earn his keep.

But London was many, many miles away. After walking twenty miles on the dusty and dirty highway that first day, Oliver sat down by the side of the road and ate his one biscuit. Then, he lay on the grass, closed his eyes, and slept.

The next day, Oliver continued walking. He found a village shop where he traded his penny for a small muffin and then spent his second night asleep by the side of the road.

Out of food and money now, Oliver walked from village to village along the highway to

London. At each village square, he humbly begged passersby for food.

In the village of Barnet, not too far from London, Oliver was nearly exhausted, so he rested for a moment on the steps of a public building. He looked across the street and saw a boy about his own age who was staring intently at him. The boy walked up to Oliver and asked, "What's the matter?"

"I haven't really eaten for days," Oliver explained, "and I'm worn out from walking nearly sixty miles."

"I suspect you are on your way to London?" the young man inquired of Oliver.

"I am."

"Well, I know someone who will give you room and board—for nothing—if I introduce the two of you. So, who are you?"

"Oliver Twist, sir."

"And I am Jack Dawkins. However, everyone calls me the 'Artful Dodger.'"

Oliver couldn't imagine what a name like "artful dodger" meant, but he followed Jack Dawkins to London. They came to an old and dirty part of town into a filthy house where an ugly, old man with thick red hair and bushy red eyebrows was roasting sausages in his kitchen fireplace.

"Oliver, meet Fagin," Jack Dawkins said.

"Fagin, meet my new pal, Oliver Twist."

It was a simple introduction. It aroused no suspicions in Oliver's mind of the ill-intentioned character of the ugly, old gentleman. Sadly, Oliver would learn this fact later.

Jack Dawkins helped himself and Oliver to a portion of the sausage. Soon, it was time for bed. Oliver slept long and sound and deep. When his eyes opened, he surveyed his new surroundings with the fuzziness of one not sure if he is awake or not.

The old man was drinking a cup of coffee and didn't know he was being observed by his new guest, whom he supposed was still asleep.

Because Fagin thought he had a quiet, private moment to himself, he took the opportunity to unlock his treasure box of precious jewelry and expensive watches. He liked the feel of the booty in his hands. Fagin cherished each piece gleefully whenever he had the chance.

Oliver sensed how strange it was for a man with such wealth to live in such a rundown, neglected house. It puzzled the boy.

Oliver washed his face using water in a basin, combed his wavy hair, and cleaned up the area by tossing the soapy water out the window—which was the custom in those days—just as the Artful Dodger and another companion climbed the steps to Fagin's front door.

Jack Dawkins, his friend, Charley Bates, Fagin, and Oliver sat around the breakfast table and ate biscuits, ham, and coffee.

The old man looked craftily at Oliver but spoke instead to the Artful Dodger and Charley, "How was the morning's work?"

"Not easy," answered Jack.

"Rather difficult, sir," Charley chimed in.

"But you were successful?" Fagin asked.

The Artful Dodger nodded in reply and brought forth two pocketbooks, each filled with a fair amount of cash. The Dodger placed the wallets in the middle of the table for Fagin's examination.

Then, the Dodger, Charley Bates, and Fagin began to play a most unusual game, which Oliver watched in amazement. First, the old man filled the pockets of his vest, jacket, and trousers with various items of value. Then, he put on a long overcoat that concealed the filled pockets. He buttoned all the buttons of the overcoat and filled the outside pockets of his overcoat with even more items.

The old man walked around the room as if he were a gentleman strolling down the village market streets. He stopped at several points in the room and pretended to look intently at each scene as a person would do when window-shopping along a row of stores.

Watching the old man carefully, the Dodger and Charley hid from his sight behind chairs or doors until just the right moment. The Dodger sprang forth to bump into Fagin as if by accident, while Charley Bates skillfully reached into the man's bulging pockets and swiped item after item of the man's possessions.

The game stopped if Fagin felt Charley's hand and could identify which pocket had been picked. The boys would be declared the losers of that particular round, and thus the game continued.

After several rounds, the play was interrupted by the arrival of a visitor: a young girl named Nancy. Charley looked at Nancy and the Dodger and commented that it must be time to go. The three youths accepted a few coins from Fagin's hand and walked out into the street.

"They did work for you, sir?" Oliver inquired of the old man.

"That they did, young Oliver, and very well, too—as you shall do if you use them as your examples. Model yourself after them, Oliver, especially the Dodger, and you will grow to be a very successful man. Here now, try to pick the handkerchief out of my pocket without my knowledge as I tidy up these cups and saucers."

Oliver repeated the actions he had just observed in the Dodger and ever so deftly removed the man's handkerchief.

"Excellent," exclaimed Fagin, as he rewarded Oliver with a shiny, new shilling.

CHAPTER 5

Not a Game

Days passed, and Oliver became bored with being cooped up in the old man's house. So, he begged Fagin to let him join the Dodger and Charley on one of their outings. Finally, Fagin gave his permission.

Oliver knew not what to expect from this outing, for his young and naive mind had not yet fully comprehended the true business his new friends practiced. For him, the outing was simply a chance to breathe some fresh air.

He was dismayed, therefore, to witness the behavior of his two companions. The Dodger walked the streets like a common bully, knocking off the hats of passing children just for the sport of it. But, even worse, Oliver saw Charley steal apples from the fruit merchant and place them in the deep pockets of his overcoat.

Oliver started to say he wanted no more part of this outing when the Dodger quickly pulled him and Charley around a corner to have a hushed conversation.

"What is it?" quivered Oliver.

"I've found the right one," said the Dodger.

Charley, understanding the Dodger's implication, asked, "Who...where is he?"

"Over there," the Dodger motioned across the street to indicate a gentleman standing by the bookstore. He was a handsome older man, dressed in fine clothes, and he was intently looking through the pages of a book he was considering purchasing.

In a matter of seconds, the Dodger and Charley rushed across the street, picked the gentleman's pocket and ran away just as they had rehearsed in Fagin's apartment. The shocking difference, however, was that this action was no game, and the innocent shopper was no player.

Oliver was so stunned he could not believe his eyes, but knowing he must flee, he turned to run in any direction he could find.

At the same moment, the gentleman swirled around and detected the fleeting motion of young Oliver.

"Stop him, stop him! He's a thief!" the man screamed to all passersby as he hurried in pursuit of the young Oliver.

Charley Bates and the Dodger, who had hidden among the crowd of shoppers, joined the chase to hide the fact that it was they, not Oliver, who had done the ugly deed.

Excitement rose as dozens joined the chase. The shouts of many voices added to the tumultuous chorus of, "Stop, stop, you little pickpocket!"

Finally, the crowd overtook poor Oliver. Someone roughly grabbed him by the collar;

and the whole crowd waited breathlessly for the gentleman to identify him.

"Is he the one who did it?"

"I'm afraid it is he."

"Afraid? Have no pity on him, sir. There's no good in him."

Oliver was hot and dirty, his lip bled from a punch he had taken from one of his captors, and he was enormously afraid.

"The poor child," said the gentleman, "he's hurt."

Just then, a policeman arrived and took Oliver into custody.

"I didn't do it, sir," Oliver said, as he was dragged along to the police station. The gentleman followed, repeating several times, "Please be careful with him. He's hurt and afraid."

At the station, the gentleman recounted the events of that day. "But I don't know if this is really the chap who stole my wallet," he emphasized. "I'd rather not press charges."

The police sergeant felt it his duty, however, to lock Oliver in a jail cell to await a hearing.

The gentleman resigned himself to wait until the proceedings commenced. He couldn't get the sweet and frightened expression of Oliver's face out of his thoughts.

That face, recollected the fine gentleman, *so innocent, it touches my heart greatly. He*

reminds me of someone...someone I've known before...but for the life of me, I know not who it is.

Soon, the gentleman, the police officer, and Oliver were brought into the court room.

"Who stands before me robbed?" the judge questioned.

"I was, your honor," the gentleman replied. "I am Mr. Brownlow."

"And who stands accused?" continued the judge.

"It is the boy, Oliver Twist," the policeman added.

"Tell me the details, sir," the judge nodded to Mr. Brownlow.

The kind gentleman proceeded to explain the events of the robbery. He stressed at every turn that Oliver may not have been the thief and asked for leniency for the boy if he was indeed found guilty. "He has been injured, your honor, and I think he is sick, besides."

In truth, Oliver was sick with confusion and terror, so much so that at that precise moment, he fainted to the floor.

The judge—perhaps hardened by seeing other cases where crafty criminals would have taken advantage of such a scene by pretending to faint away—was not moved by the orphan's very real distress. He convicted Oliver to three months in jail.

The court aides were ready to carry out the limp body of the boy, who was still passed out, when the court room door flew open and an elderly shopkeeper hurried to the judge's bench.

"Wait," implored the shopkeeper. "He is not the thief. I saw the whole event, and it is two other boys who should be standing here accused."

"What took you so long in providing this testimony?" the judge demanded.

"I had no one to look after my bookstore, your honor. Everyone, sir, all my customers

and clerks, ran out to follow the commotion and left me stranded behind. I have come as soon as I could."

"I accept your eyewitness account." The judge then pounded his gavel upon the bench and declared, "The boy may go free."

Mr. Brownlow gently picked up the pale and trembling Oliver, who was reviving, and cradled him in his arm.

"Someone call a coach for us, please," directed the gentleman.

"May I help carry the boy?" the shopkeeper offered.

"Bless you, sir."

The coach arrived, and the two gentlemen, with Oliver between them, rode to Mr. Brownlow's tidy home in Pentonville, one of London's prettiest neighborhoods.

CHAPTER 6

The Portrait

Oliver was made comfortable in Mr. Brownlow's home, in a bed of such softness he had never felt and among kindness he had never known. He slept for days, his body racked with fever, proving that Mr. Brownlow had assumed correctly that Oliver Twist was, indeed, quite ill. A sweet, grandmotherly woman sat at Oliver's bedside constantly watching for his care. Mrs. Bedwin's hands stitched a delicate embroidery as her heart and ears listened for clues of Oliver's health.

At last, his trembling voice was heard to ask, "Where am I?"

Lovingly, Mrs. Bedwin felt his forehead to determine its temperature. Oliver grasped hold of her hand, responding to the first motherly care he had ever received.

"Sweet child," the woman spoke, "how grateful your own mother would feel now if she were here."

"I think she is here," Oliver whispered. "I sense her presence often, and I have seen her beautiful face in my dreams many times."

Mrs. Bedwin gave Oliver a sip of cool water and advised him to continue his rest. A few hours later, Oliver opened his eyes to see that Mrs. Bedwin had called in a doctor.

The doctor held Oliver's wrist with his right hand and timed the boy's pulse by counting it according to the noisy ticking of an expensive, gold watch that he held in his left hand.

"Ummm...," said the doctor, "you are feeling well, aren't you?"

"Yes, much better," Oliver said cheerfully.

"Certainly, I knew you were and you are hungry."

"No, not really," Oliver replied.

"Undoubtedly not!" the doctor returned. "I knew you would certainly not be hungry."

"But you are tired and need a nap," the doctor continued, desperately trying to recall every ounce of medical diagnosis he could find to display his wisdom.

"No, I feel quite rested, thank you, sir," Oliver commented.

"No, not tired, either," confirmed the doctor. "Of course not, I did not think you were! But you are thirsty, are you not?"

"Oh, yes, quite, sir!" Oliver answered.

"Exactly as I thought!" the doctor said jubilantly! Relieved that he could leave now, the doctor proceeded—with a self-important air—to tell Mrs. Bedwin what she already knew. Oliver was better!

That night, after sleeping for a few hours, Oliver awoke and was not certain of where he was nor why. He looked around the room and realized that he had almost died. Grateful, but knowing that he still was not completely well, Oliver thanked the Lord and humbly prayed for strength.

After three days, Oliver was strong enough to come downstairs to eat supper in Mrs. Bedwin's kitchen.

As Mrs. Bedwin placed a steaming bowl of hearty vegetable soup at the child's place, she saw him staring at a portrait on the wall.

The picture was of a young woman whose wavy, auburn hair was held away from her face by two silver barrettes. At her throat was a golden locket attached to a velvet ribbon. Her pale blue gown draped softly over her shoulders.

"Do you like the portrait, child?" Mrs. Bedwin asked.

"Yes, I like it very much. Who is she?"

"I never heard who she is, dear. She certainly does not look like anyone I know," Mrs. Bedwin told the child.

Oliver studied the painting intently and commented, "She is a very pretty lady." Then, he added softly, "But her eyes are so sad, they seem to look right at me. It's as if she wants to tell me something."

"What do you mean?" Then, Mrs. Bedwin, concerned that Oliver's fever was returning and was making him imagine things, quickly pushed his chair around so that he would not look directly upon the haunting picture.

Oliver ate with good appetite. Just as he finished the last scrumptious spoonful of Mrs. Bedwin's soup, a knock came on the kitchen door.

"Yes," answered the housekeeper.

Mr. Brownlow entered the room. "How are you, child?" the kind gentleman asked.

"Happy, sir, and ever so thankful to you," Oliver replied with a sweet and bright look that nearly lit up the room.

Once again, there was something in his face that jarred Mr. Brownlow's memories.

Where have I seen those features before? he questioned himself, and as he did so, his eyes fixed upon the portrait on the wall.

So startled was he by the resemblance between the beautiful lady in the picture and the sweet orphan at his table, that he jerked his head and gasped.

His sudden reaction frightened Oliver, who thinking he had somehow displeased the kind man and being not fully recovered from his illness, fainted once more in his chair.

For several more days, Oliver continued to rest. These days were most pleasant. Mrs. Bedwin taught him how to play cribbage and entertained him with stories of her own children. This quiet, peaceful way of life was so different from the dreadful turmoil Oliver had endured all his life, that Oliver guessed it must be a lot like Heaven.

CHAPTER 7

A Parrot Man

As soon as Oliver was well enough to shop for some new clothes, Mr. Brownlow took him to the tailor's and purchased a new velvet suit, a new hat, and new shoes. Oliver had never had new clothes before. He gave his old clothes to one of Mr. Brownlow's kitchen servants and suggested she sell them at the trader's shop so that she could make some money to buy anything she wanted.

One evening, Mr. Brownlow asked to see Oliver alone in his study. The study contained more books than Oliver had ever seen.

"You have my permission to read anything you wish," the old gentleman offered.

"I'm grateful to you, sir...for so many things," Oliver replied.

"I know you are, child." Mr. Brownlow removed his gold glasses and looked directly at Oliver. "Now listen," he continued, "we have some important business to discuss."

Seeing Mr. Brownlow's serious expression, Oliver jumped to an alarming conclusion. "Please don't send me away, sir. I'll work for my keep. I can be your servant."

"Sweet child, I have no intention of abandoning you—unless you give me a reason to do so."

"I won't sir—never!"

"I trust you, Oliver. It is true that a few times before, I have had my trust broken. But there is something about you—although I don't know what it is—that stirs my heart. My heart has been wounded, Oliver, for you see, everyone I have ever loved has now died, and I am left alone."

The gentleman continued, "It is clear that sorrow has wounded you, child. Will you tell me what happened? Friends are not afraid to share their deepest thoughts."

Oliver began to tell his sad story when a knock came on the front door.

The servant announced to Mr. Brownlow that Mr. Grimwig had come for tea.

"Should I leave now," Oliver asked, "so that you may visit with your friend?"

"No, Oliver. I'd like the two of you to meet. I think you will find my friend most interesting though at times he can be a bit rough around the edges," Mr. Brownlow said with a chuckle.

Mr. Grimwig entered the study, was introduced to Oliver, and proceeded to chat with his old friend.

As they talked, Oliver found much amusement in watching a strange mannerism the visitor displayed. Every so often, Mr. Grimwig would turn his head to the side, look out the corners of his eyes and remark, "If it isn't so, I'll eat my head." He looked like a parrot, and Oliver had never seen anything like it before.

Then, Mr. Brownlow asked Oliver to check to see if the tea and biscuits were ready for his guest. While Oliver was out of the room, Mr. Brownlow asked his friend what he thought of the boy.

Mr. Grimwig, in a rather disagreeable mood that evening, decided to warn his friend of every possible danger in bringing an unknown orphan into one's home.

"If I were you, Brownlow, I would have your housekeeper count the silver every night after Oliver goes to bed. If there's not something missing someday, I'll eat my head!"

Mr. Brownlow didn't mind this disagreeable remark, for he was well acquainted with his friend's odd habits. And when Oliver returned with hot tea and warm cakes, Mr. Grimwig practiced better manners by complimenting Mr. Brownlow on the delicious refreshment. Thus, Oliver found himself quite comfortable until, that is, Mr. Grimwig started asking him about his past.

"When will you be confiding in the good Mr. Brownlow the details of your life's story, my young man?"

Mr. Brownlow interrupted, for he felt Oliver's upbringing was something he wanted to hear in private from the youngster, so he explained, "We're going to discuss things tomorrow. I'm

sure Oliver will tell me all I need to know, won't you, Oliver?"

"I shall, sir."

"I wouldn't be so sure, Brownlow," his friend, who liked to be contradictory, remarked.

"I believe him!" Mr. Brownlow's irritation was rising as was Mr. Grimwig's. It was convenient that at that very moment, Mrs. Bedwin announced that a delivery boy had just come with Mr. Brownlow's order of new books.

She handed the books to the old gentleman and was about to leave when Mr. Brownlow called her back.

"Wait, Mrs. Bedwin, I didn't order one of these books. Has the delivery boy already left?"

"Yes, sir."

"Oh, dear, I don't wish to keep a book without paying for it. I'll have to settle my account tomorrow."

"Have Oliver pay your bill tonight," Mr. Grimwig suggested with a gleam in his eye. "It will be a test of his honest character."

Mr. Brownlow, happy to prove the child's trustworthiness replied, "Yes, Oliver, will you take this five-pound note to the shopkeeper for me tonight, dear—and wait for him to give you ten shillings in change."

"Yes, sir, and I'll be quick about it, sir."

Mrs. Bedwin gave Oliver careful directions to find the Pentonville bookstore, and she stood in the doorway to watch Oliver until he was out of sight.

"You actually think he will return?" Mr. Grimwig asked his host.

"Of course, why wouldn't he come back?"

"He's wearing the fine new clothes you bought him; he has your money in his hand...I venture to say he'll seek out his gang of thieves and forget he ever met you. Why, if he comes back, I'll eat my head!"

CHAPTER 8

Trapped Again

The web of criminals which Oliver had naively stumbled upon consisted not only of the Artful Dodger, Charley Bates, and Nancy, but also several other youths who all worked for Fagin. And Fagin, himself, worked under an even more dangerous character named Bill Sikes.

One evening, Mr. Sikes and Nancy were walking down the street, talking over the matter of the missing Oliver when whom should they see sauntering merrily upon his way to a bookstore, but Oliver Twist himself!

Oliver was traveling along in a peaceful, contented mood, appreciating so much his new

circumstances. His only wish was that he could see his friend, Dick, once more and know that life had taken a better turn for him also.

Quick as lightning, the two criminals grabbed the boy right off his feet and whisked him away. Oliver kicked and screamed but to no avail. No passerby was interested in helping him. So, he was caught in the terrible trap once more and knew not where his kidnappers were carrying him.

Mr. Sikes and Nancy led the boy through a few dark and narrow streets until they came to a dirty and run down old apartment house. The entryway was so dark that Oliver didn't recognize who had unchained the door for them until he heard the voice: It was the Artful Dodger.

The scoundrel led them to a musty-smelling kitchen. Charley Bates was sitting by the fire with Fagin, who had returned a few minutes earlier. They looked at the boy as Oliver stared at them in utter amazement.

"What fine clothes he's wearing!" Charley Bates whistled. "We have a real fine gentleman, here, that's what we have...and look what's in his pocket. If it isn't a five-pound note and some pretty books. My, my, aren't we coming up in the world?" mocked Charley.

"No, no," pleaded Oliver. "The money isn't mine. It's Mr. Brownlow's. Send it back to him, please. I don't care what you do to me, but please send his money back to him."

Oliver was brokenhearted, for he knew the kind, old gentleman would think he had run off to keep the money for himself.

There must be a way to escape, thought the boy. Then, seeing his chance to flee, Oliver suddenly ran for the bolted door. However, he was quickly overtaken by the three who were determined not to lose sight of him again. Only Nancy, regretting the life they were pulling Oliver into and wishing he had been successful in his attempted flight, screamed at Sikes, Fagin, and Charley Bates.

"Let him alone! Let him go!"

Her face turned white with anger and she became so enraged that she bit her lip and cried, "What horrible men are you to try to make a liar and a thief out of this young boy?"

"And who are you to be judging the likes of us?" Bill Sikes demanded.

"I know, I know," Nancy shrieked, "you have turned me into something even worse!" And, at that outburst, Nancy fainted to the floor.

Sikes laid her in a corner of the room and ordered Charley to show Oliver where he could sleep. Charley gleefully accepted the assignment, for it gave him the devious pleasure of showing Oliver the pile of used clothes they had placed on an old cot awaiting his return. They were Oliver's old suit of clothes. Fagin had spotted them at the trader's shop and concluded correctly that the orphan-boy must be somewhere in the vicinity.

"Change into your old rags, little boy," directed Charley. "You'll need them for tomor-

row's work, and Fagin will see to these rich ones."

Oliver did as he was told, then in helpless desperation, he fell upon the cot and slept until morning. And all this time, Mr. Brownlow, Mr. Grimwig, and Mrs. Bedwin sat in the shadows of candlelight waiting for his return.

A day later, Mr. Bumble happened to be visiting London on business. He checked into an inn to spend the night and then treated himself to some refreshment. He ordered a cup of tea and glanced at a newspaper that someone had left behind.

There on the front page was a notice of reward provided for anyone who could give information about the whereabouts or history of one Oliver Twist! The advertisement was signed by Mr. Brownlow and noted his address.

Mr. Bumble made haste to the Pentonville home, where a servant girl speedily opened the door upon hearing the official mention the name of Oliver Twist. She led Mr. Bumble to the study where Mr. Brownlow and Mr. Grimwig were talking.

"Do you have knowledge of Oliver's whereabouts, sir?" Mr. Brownlow inquired of Mr. Bumble with great anticipation.

"No, I do not."

"Then, what can you tell me about him?"

Mr. Bumble settled comfortably in his chair and took twenty minutes to give an account that contained the following remarks:

"Oliver is an orphan, a child of parents who were good for nothing, I assume. He was ungratefully discontent with all the provision the workhouse staff gave him. When placed in an apprenticeship, he picked a fight with an innocent young man, and then ran away from the perfectly good home and the perfectly good job."

Mr. Brownlow, in great disappointment and sadness, paid Mr. Bumble the reward money and bid him good night.

Mr. Grimwig remained and added to Mr. Brownlow's grief by reminding him that he, Mr. Grimwig, had warned him that the boy was no good.

Mrs. Bedwin, who had been called to the study as soon as Mr. Bumble left and informed of the story, defended the child. "I cannot believe there is a mean bone in his body, sir. Please hold out hope for him, sir."

"No, Mrs. Bedwin. I am through with Oliver Twist. We will not speak his name again, not ever!"

CHAPTER 9

The Dreadful Plan

Back in Barrington Alley, Fagin spent a great deal of the next day frightening Oliver with the threat that if he ever ran away again, Fagin would see to it that the boy was hanged.

After the lecture, Fagin locked Oliver in a room and left him there for days. All the while, Oliver's thoughts were with Mr. Brownlow and Mrs. Bedwin and with what sad thoughts they must be having of him.

Fagin continued brainwashing Oliver to convince him that he was a common thief just like the rest of them and that the orphan's best course was to pay attention to their training in crime.

Weeks later, although Fagin was not entirely certain that Oliver had converted to the ways of criminals, Fagin decided that the boy could be used in a housebreaking job! The house he and Sikes had targeted to break into had a tiny, unsecured window that only a small lad like Oliver could squeeze through.

Fagin announced to Oliver that in a few hours, he would be turned over to Mr. Sikes, but he did not tell Oliver why.

Then, perhaps to harden Oliver's skin—or soul—Fagin ordered Oliver to read a book that told the stories of criminals and their deadly deeds. Fagin left the house but told Oliver to read the dreadful book until someone arrived to fetch him for the day's journey.

The stories were appalling. In fear and desperation, Oliver threw the book to the floor, folded his trembling hands in prayer and whis-

pered, "Oh, Lord, I do not want to be a criminal. Please rescue me. I would rather die than commit these wicked deeds."

Just then, he heard a noise at the front door. It was Nancy unlocking the door. She was nervous and looked as if she might faint.

"Sit down, Nancy. What is it?"

"I'm so sorry, Oliver. I never thought I'd pull in someone as sweet as you...." Her voice trailed off.

Then, she stiffened her back, resigned herself to her unwanted task, and said with as little emotion as possible, "Come with me, I am to take you to Sikes."

Even the name of Sikes terrified the boy, but he reasoned that if, at least, he got out of the locked residence, then perhaps he could also free himself from Nancy and run away to safety.

Nancy seemed to read the orphan's thoughts. "Oliver, if you run from me, they will beat me even more than they have done to

make me come to get you." She lifted her sleeve and showed Oliver the black and blue bruises she had already sustained.

Oliver swallowed hard, took her hand, and quietly followed Nancy out to her waiting coach. They rode in silence to Bill Sikes' apartment.

Once inside, Sikes greeted them heartily, but became quite serious as he informed Oliver of the behavior he demanded. "Do you see this pistol?" Sikes inquired.

Oliver nodded, but before he could say anything, Sikes pointed the gun at the boy's forehead and snarled, "And do you know what happens when I pull this trigger? Because that's exactly what I will do if you make a peep when we're on this job tonight—unless I directly ask you a question. Do you understand?"

"Yes, sir."

"Now we need to get some sleep. Nancy, awaken us at 2 a.m. and not a minute later."

Mr. Sikes went to his bedroom, Nancy sat by the fireplace, and Oliver settled on a nearby cot.

Soon it was the appointed time. For hours, they walked through the cold, dark streets of London. Even when the black night began to fade into morning, it was a cloudy, gloomy day that dawned upon the city.

Slowly, the town's inhabitants began to awaken. Burning candles and lighted gas-lamps appeared behind the windows of the shops and apartments that they were passing on this journey to no good end.

Wagon loads of fruits and vegetables were arriving from the countryside, fishermen carried in large baskets filled with fish from the night's catch, the cattlemen led carts of livestock to the butchers, and the wives of dairy men carried heavy pails of fresh milk into the market square.

It was a busy morning for everyone; but sadly, Oliver's business was to trudge along beside the shameless Mr. Bill Sikes.

They walked all day until it was night again. There was no moon. Again, it was dark, cold, and rainy. Sikes led Oliver quickly through the outskirts of London until they finally came to a meeting place where his accomplice, Toby Crackit, awaited their arrival. Toby muttered, "Who's the boy?"

"He's Oliver Twist, one of Fagin's boys."

Later that night, the three hurried toward the countryside, crossed a bridge to the locale of Chertsey, and came to a large estate where a stone wall surrounded a stately mansion.

Toby, who was young and nimble, easily climbed to the top of the wall and directed Sikes in lifting the boy up to him. Sikes then followed, a little more slowly, but successfully; and soon all three were inside the garden wall.

Oliver's stomach twisted in panic as he suddenly realized he was to be part of a housebreaking!

"No, I won't do this," Oliver wailed.

Sikes drew his pistol from his pocket, but Toby knocked it away. Toby covered Oliver's mouth with his huge, rough hands, yanked the boy along, and assured Sikes he would keep Oliver quiet.

They approached the house that had been scouted out ahead of time and located the window shutter the criminals knew was loose. The two men forced the shutter open with a crowbar. This gained access to a small window too small for either Sikes or Toby to enter, but not too small for Oliver to crawl through.

Sikes shined lantern-light on Oliver's face and spoke sternly to him, "After I lift you through that window, I'll pass this lantern in. You walk through the hallway to the front door and unlock it so we can get in. I warn you, I'll have this gun aimed on you all the way."

In the few seconds it took Sikes to make this speech, Oliver had time to devise his own plan. He decided that even if he were shot in

the process, once he was inside the house, he would run to wherever the residents were sleeping and awaken them.

So, as soon as Oliver's feet touched the inside floor, he put down his lantern and started to run up a nearby staircase.

"No, Oliver, no!" Sikes yelled.

Another scream was heard, Oliver knew not from where.

Two men appeared across the room from him. A gunshot.

The impact of the piercing bullet threw Oliver backward. There was utter confusion as the parties inside the mansion and the criminals on the outside panicked in the darkness. Sikes ripped open the remaining shutter and somehow managed to gather the wounded boy. He carried Oliver outside and joined Toby in scampering away.

But when the house residents began to chase the robbers with guard dogs, Sikes dropped the now unconscious Oliver into a

muddy ditch. Bill Sikes ran away in one direction, and Toby Crackit fled in another.

Agnes
1821

CHAPTER 10

A Golden Locket

Back in the town where Oliver had been born, Widow Corney, a maid in the workhouse, was preparing a pot of tea. As she poured boiling water into the small teapot, which was all she needed for the solitary cup of tea she would drink, the water overflowed the teapot's rim and burned her fingers. The hot pain sadly reminded Mrs. Corney of how lonely it is to live alone.

Just then, from her apartment door, a knock was heard that Mrs. Corney did not appreciate. She assumed it was one of the old paupers calling for some dreaded assistance—and timed just as always—to interrupt her afternoon tea!

"Oh, enter, if you must," the widow called in unkind exasperation.

However, the widow was most surprised to see that the caller was Mr. Bumble, the workhouse official, who was making what would seem to be a business visit.

"It is frightfully cold outside, ma'am."

"That it is. Won't you have a spot of warm tea with me, Mr. Bumble?"

They sat around the table in front of the fireplace. They sipped their tea, munched on toast, and looked tenderly into one another's eyes.

Mr. Bumble was about to engage in a rather sentimental conversation (for romance, of a sort, was the true business he intended) and one that Mrs. Corney would, no doubt, have welcomed and encouraged, when another knock was heard on her door.

The caller did not wait for Mrs. Corney to reply but opened the door herself and cried, "You must come quickly. Sally is dying, and she's begging to see you first."

Perturbed at the interruption dealing with one of the paupers, Mrs. Corney asked Mr. Bumble to wait for her return. She threw on her woolen shawl and ran impatiently after the caller.

Mr. Bumble did not mind waiting in the slightest. Indeed, it gave him a chance to enjoy himself by surveying the widow's belongings: her silver forks, pewter bowls, and china plates—and he was quite pleased with what he saw.

Mrs. Corney and her guide made their way to the sick woman's room in the attic of the workhouse. The frail woman's face was drawn tight with pain, and she struggled to speak to Mrs. Corney.

"Come close, so you can hear me," the dying woman's words faltered. "I have little strength to speak."

She painfully continued, "Ten or eleven years ago, a beautiful young woman died in this same bed after having had a baby boy."

"Why are you telling me this, Sally?"

"Because... I stole the gold from her. I must confess it before I die! She wore rags and was starving, but she had protected a golden locket. She trusted the gold to me—to give to her child—but I kept it for myself. Mrs. Corney, my friend, you must find the boy for me and return his property to him."

"Who is he and where can I find him?"

"All I remember is that he was named Oliver Twist...and his mother's locket is...." Sally's voice trailed off, she closed her eyes, and died.

Back in London, Fagin waited impatiently for the housebreakers' return. Finally, the door opened, but only Toby Crackit was there.

"Where are Sikes and the orphan?" Fagin demanded.

"The job was a bust," Toby spoke, his expression absent of expression. "They shot

the boy, and we had to escape any way we could. They were chasing us with attack dogs, Fagin. I don't know any more."

The old man was outraged! He ran from his house and out into the streets! Fagin paid for a coach ride to Sikes' apartment to see if he had come home by now. He entered and found, however, that Nancy was still anxiously waiting for the housebreakers to return. When Fagin told Nancy the account he had heard from Toby, despair and remorse filled her heart.

Fagin tried to console the girl. "I am sorry for the boy," he said.

"Sorry? He's better off dead than among the likes of us!" Nancy cried. "And as for Bill Sikes...I hope he was murdered also. Now leave me to my grief!"

At that outcry, Fagin departed. When he approached his rundown apartment, it was quite late and dark and cold. As he neared the entrance, he was startled by an ugly man cloaked in black who was hiding in the shadows.

Fagin was startled, but not surprised. The two entered the apartment. As soon as Fagin closed the door, the stranger reacted with fear of the darkness and the enclosed space and yelled, "Get a light. Get a light or I will knock my head against a wall."

Fagin lit a candle, and they began to talk in whispers so as not to awaken Jack Dawkins, Charley Bates, and Toby Crackit who were asleep. The whispers became louder, however, as the two began to argue.

The voice of the stranger, whom Fagin called, "Monks," then rose to make the following accusation. "It was a stupid plan! You should not have sent that boy. I only asked you to make him a pickpocket and nothing more! If the boy is dead, I am not responsible, do you hear me Fagin? Do you hear?" the stranger stammered as he drew his black cloak around him and stormed out into the night.

CHAPTER 11

A Fine Home

And on this same night, Mr. Bumble remained in Mrs. Corney's parlor patiently awaiting her return. Mr. Bumble, however, did not mind the time alone. As stated earlier, Mr. Bumble was possessed of a rather high and exaggerated opinion of himself. He had determined to acquire for himself the appearances of a mighty fine home: the kind of pampered surroundings that were, no doubt, his due.

So, he counted and recounted the widow's household belongings. He even opened drawers and closets and made a mental inventory of all her domestic wealth.

Suddenly, Mrs. Corney, in an agitated state, bounded into the room. "Oh, what a dreadful evening," she wailed.

"What has upset you so, my dear?" Mr. Bumble asked as he handed Mrs. Corney a cup of tea to soothe her nerves.

Mrs. Corney sipped the warm liquid, heaved a sigh, and replied, "I'll be alright shortly."

"Relax, dear. You are in the comfort of your own home now, and I am here besides. It is a lovely apartment, Mrs. Corney. If there were one more room, it would be a fine home, indeed," he said with a twinkle in his eye.

"And what would a woman alone need with more room, sir?"

"A little more space would be just right for two, my love, do you agree?"

Mrs. Corney blushed and put her hand in his.

Sweet sentimentality, however, did not distract Mr. Bumble from monetary calculations, and he asked, "Your monthly allowance does

include coals for the fireplace and plenty of candles, does it not, Mrs. Corney?"

"Oh, yes, Mr. Bumble!"

Upon hearing all this good news, Mr. Bumble could no longer refrain from hugging Mrs. Corney. So, he did, and kissed her, too!

"Your workhouse supervisor is on his deathbed, Mrs. Corney, and when he is gone, I can apply for his position and move here—that is if you will agree to marry me."

"I will," the widow answered quickly.

The matter thus decided, the blushing couple poured themselves another cup of tea and conversed about the night's events at old Sally's bedside.

Cold rain continued through the dark night and fell on Oliver as he lay passed out in the ditch; but finally, morning brought another day.

The throbbing sensation in Oliver's shoulder brought the boy to his senses, and he cried out in pain. He opened his eyes to see his blood-soaked shirt. Weak and full of terror, Oliver's survival instincts told him he must find help as quickly as possible.

The orphan-boy staggered and stumbled but made his way to the very house his unsavory companions had tried to rob the night before. The sight of the house and the thought of what its occupants must think of him terrified the boy, but he reasoned: where else could he go?

There was only enough strength left in the boy to knock softly on the side door before he collapsed on the porch.

A butler, Mr. Giles, and Brittles, a servant, were in the kitchen relating the night's frightening excitement to the cooks and housemaids. The servants were so engrossed in the tale of these two brave men who had chased off villainous robbers, that Oliver's knock—soft as it was—startled the group into a frozen panic.

"Someone, go to the door," Mr. Giles said as he nodded toward Brittles.

"Oh, I don't think I can, sir," answered the servant, who had had quite enough excitement the night before.

So, deciding there was safety in numbers, the whole group walked to the door and timidly opened it just a crack.

"Why, it's only a child," gasped Mr. Giles.

"It's the boy you shot last night!" Brittles exclaimed.

"Tell the Miss and Madam that we've captured the robber!" someone cried.

However, the young lady of the house was already rushing into the room, and her sweet voice was heard to say, "Is he hurt badly?"

"Frightfully, Miss Rose," Brittles answered. "I think he is dying."

"Carry him carefully to the guest bedroom, someone...and you, Brittles, fetch the doctor quickly," the beautiful lady directed.

Within an hour, Dr. Losberne arrived and attended to the boy's wounds while Miss Rose and the owner of the mansion, whom she called Aunt Maylie, waited anxiously in the parlor.

After removing the bullet from Oliver's shoulder and bandaging his arm, the surgeon called the ladies into the sick child's room. Oliver lay asleep, his delicate body seeming far too frail to have withstood the relentless tragedies of the past eleven years.

The doctor lamented to the ladies, "It distresses me greatly, my dears, to know that in the middle of the night, robbers broke into your house! I can't imagine how bold the criminal mind must be!"

Miss Rose, especially tenderhearted, looked upon the boy with great compassion and declared, "Oh, this young man cannot be a hardened criminal. There must be some mistake."

"Perhaps so," agreed the equally kind-hearted doctor, "we shall learn more when he awakens."

Several hours later, Oliver did open his eyes and gazed upon the pure and gentle face of Miss Rose. Her golden hair was braided into rings atop her head, her blue eyes danced with intelligence and happiness, and her pink brocade dress swished softly as she walked.

Sensing the protection presented to him by these three—the lovely young woman, the doctor, and Mrs. Maylie—Oliver pleaded for their mercy. With shortness of breath and terror in his eyes, he recounted to them the events of his entire life and convinced them of his innocence.

Miss Rose reacted first and spoke to her aunt, "Oh, Aunt Maylie, if I had not received your love and care when I, myself, was such a helpless child, my future might be as bleak as this young man's seems to be today."

Then, Miss Rose implored both the doctor and her aunt, "We must discover how we can save him."

So, Oliver's story was accepted with Christian compassion. Everyone determined to offer the boy whatever protection he needed, so that the rest of his life would be far happier than what he had thus far experienced.

CHAPTER 12

Summer in the Country

And so the boy recovered in the Maylie home from his broken arm and the fever brought on by the night in the drenching rain. He was so grateful to Miss Rose and Mrs. Maylie that he daily asked things he could do for them to show his thankfulness.

"I would stand on my head for you, dear Miss Rose, if it would make you happy!" Oliver spoke with the exuberance of a youth whose strength had returned.

Oliver's prayers of thankfulness brought blessings upon the entire household, and his sweet ambitions delighted the ladies.

"Oliver, your gratefulness makes me very happy," Miss Rose smiled beautifully as she spoke.

"I am so glad that it does," Oliver responded.

"Do you suppose I could also someday make Mr. Brownlow and Mrs. Bedwin happy, too? They were so very good to me."

"When you are well enough, dear Oliver, I will send you on a visit to Mr. Brownlow and you may thank him all you like."

Oliver was ecstatic!

Several days later, Dr. Losberne reported that Oliver was, indeed, strong enough for the trip. So the doctor and the orphan-boy boarded a coach to London.

Oliver instructed the coach driver with excellent directions, and they soon pulled up outside the Pemberton residence. The memory of this place had sustained Oliver's courage all during his captivity with Mr. Bill Sikes.

Oliver could hardly wait for the chance to explain his sudden departure from the kindness and trust of good Mr. Brownlow so many weeks ago. It pained Oliver grievously that the man might now certainly think of him as a common thief.

Yet, even that pain was not as sharp as the disappointment that stabbed Oliver's heart when he stepped out of the coach and saw that the house was vacant.

"They are gone!" Oliver gasped, as his face turned pale with shock.

Dr. Losberne was just as surprised. "What could have become of them?" he wondered aloud. He stepped out of the coach and inquired of the neighbors for the whereabouts of Mr. Brownlow and his servants, especially Mrs. Bedwin.

"They have moved to the West Indies, sir. We're not sure exactly where."

The only thing Oliver and Dr. Losberne could do was to turn around and start back the way they came. As they rode back to the estate in Chertsey, Oliver's thoughts darted

from one miserable question to the next. *How could it be that he would never see Mr. Brownlow and Mrs. Bedwin again? Would he never get a chance to explain his circumstances to them? Would he ever be permitted to find happiness? Where would life carry him next?*

The last question was answered in a few days when Miss Rose announced that the entire household would spend the summer months at the country cottage. For the first time in his life, Oliver had the pleasure of breathing clear, fresh air, of smelling fragrant wildflowers, and of running through luscious, country meadows.

Not only was the country a place of pleasant rest and relaxation for the orphan-boy, but it was also a time of academic education. Oliver learned to read better and to write. He listened to Miss Rose play the piano—melodies he had never heard before. Best of all, he attended services in the village church where

Oliver found the new pleasure of worshiping with true believers. As Oliver and the two ladies walked to Sunday services, Oliver carried the Bible proudly.

Oliver was learning about human affection, too. His life was now filled with the joyous love he felt for the Maylies, which intertwined with the bountiful love they gave to him. Their hearts were linked together so strongly that it seemed nothing could break the bond until one evening, as Miss Rose played the piano, she began to cry.

"Whatever is the matter, dear?" Mrs. Maylie asked with alarm.

"I don't know, but I feel faint," Miss Rose answered with a trembling voice. "I think I'll rest for a moment."

Oliver and Mrs. Maylie gently helped Miss Rose to her bed and watched in horror as all the color drained from the young lady's face. Then, just as quickly, her face grew warm with fever. Though she tried to speak, her words could not be understood. The strange sickness continued through the night. Oliver and Mrs. Maylie cared for Miss Rose constantly, but none of their ministrations seemed to help.

When morning came and Miss Rose was no better, Mrs. Maylie frantically instructed Oliver, "You must run as fast as you can to the village post and mail this note to Dr. Losberne...and this other note too...no, I shall not post this letter unless the worst happens." Mrs. Maylie tucked one of the envelopes in her pocket and handed the one addressed to Dr. Losberne to Oliver.

"Hurry, Oliver, we must have the doctor."

Oliver would have let nothing stop him, not even a mysterious man clothed in a long, black cloak. Oliver almost ran into him as he breathlessly rounded the corner into the village. Oliver apologized to the man and said, "Excuse me, please."

The irritated stranger responded by raising his fist at Oliver as if to strike him hard.

"I did not mean to bump into you, sir." Oliver choked back alarm and tried to go around the fellow, who was now deliberately blocking the boy's way.

The man cursed Oliver and then began to shake with so much anger that his whole body convulsed, and he fell into a heap of uncontrollable tremors.

Shaking himself from this mysterious fright, Oliver continued on his way. He arrived at the post just in time to meet the rider who could carry the desperate call for help to Dr. Losberne's office in Chertsey.

"Deliver this at once!" Oliver said breathlessly as he handed his package to the rider. "Dr. Losborne must receive this right away! It's an emergency!"

Yet, in spite of Oliver's haste, it would be another day before the doctor could possibly arrive. Another day of chills and fever for Miss Rose and frustration and anxiety for Mrs. Maylie and Oliver.

During all these agonizing hours, Mrs. Maylie acted bravely on the outside while on the inside she struggled with the recognition that there was little hope. Oliver knew it, too, and so did Dr. Losberne when, on the next day, he sped into the cottage and examined the very sick young lady.

Oliver prayed more earnestly than he had ever prayed before. The hours ticked on. There was nothing more any of them could do but wait. Oliver and Mrs. Maylie did little but sit and stare into space. At meal times, the servants brought them food to eat, but nothing stirred their appetites. Their thoughts were so far away, in fact, that by the third day, they both jumped with nervous tension when Dr. Losberne entered the dining room.

When Mrs. Maylie saw the doctor and could see that he had a report to give, Mrs. Maylie could hold back her fear no longer, and she wailed, "Oh, Dr. Losborne—she is dead, isn't she?"

"No, my dear," the doctor's voice quivered with emotion. "Heaven has graciously given us her recovery. Let us thank Him now."

CHAPTER 13

Welcome and Unwelcome Guests

The next morning, Oliver ran to the woods to pick a bouquet of wildflowers for Miss Rose. His head was full of wonderful ways to express his affection for her and his thankfulness to God.

So absorbed was he in these delicious plans, that he almost did not notice a small carriage whose horses were trotting so quickly, they could have knocked him over if he had not swiftly moved out of the way.

One of the passengers, upon seeing Oliver, commanded that the carriage be stopped, and he yelled to Oliver, "I beg of you, how is Miss Rose?"

Oliver recognized the speaker's face immediately and exclaimed, "Giles!"

Then a stranger's face appeared from inside the vehicle and cried with even greater impatience, "How is Rose?"

"She is recovering, sir," Oliver gladly announced.

The unknown gentleman wiped tears from his eyes and said to Giles, "Go ahead to my mother's now, and tell her I am coming soon. I shall walk the rest of the way with this child."

The stranger who had spoken of Mrs. Maylie as "mother" said no more as he and Oliver walked on. Oliver learned nothing further until they neared the cottage where Mrs. Maylie was straining to see the first glimpse of this new guest. Then, comparing her features to the young man's appearance, Oliver could easily see how very much they looked alike. This was, indeed, Mrs. Maylie's son.

"Why didn't you write me sooner?" he cried.

Mrs. Maylie answered with slow and deliberate words, "I wrote you a lengthy letter earlier, Harry, and I almost mailed it...but, then I had a change of mind...I am sure you understand why."

"I may understand, but I do not agree. Mother, she may have died before I had had a chance to see my love once more! You will let me see her now?" the young Mr. Maylie pleaded.

"Yes," Mrs. Maylie promised, "as soon as she is able to receive visitors. Make yourself comfortable in the guest room."

Harry Maylie unpacked his suitcase in the guest room, Giles looked after the carriage horses in the stables, and Oliver retired to his room.

He planned to do his studies for awhile before dinner, but the weather was hot and Oliver was tired, so his head nodded in sleep. He began to dream—or at least he thought he was dreaming—and he saw the ugly face of

Fagin. The scene so frightened Oliver, that he shook his head, opened his eyes and saw, in fact, the faces of two men looking at him through the window. One terrifying face was that of Fagin and the other belonged to the cloaked man Oliver had run into near the village post.

"Help! Help!" cried Oliver.

The two intruders escaped into the woods. Harry Maylie and Mr. Giles responded to Oliver's cries and ran into the woods to overtake the unwelcome visitors, but no trace of their trail could be found.

For the next several days, the Maylie household cautiously watched the safety of young Oliver while at the same time they cheerfully observed the return of health to Miss Rose. Her recovery brightened everyone's spirits and gave Harry Maylie enough confidence one day to hold a long-hoped for conversation with the fair young lady.

They met in the parlor. Harry held Rose's hand and gently remarked, "Surely you know my feelings for you, dear Rose—how I have loved you since my youth."

"Speak not of it, sweet Harry. You must find someone else to love."

"Why do you hold this devastating opinion?" the young man implored.

"Because a future with me as your wife would be ruinous for your career plans. You are bound for fame and great status. My humble background does not qualify me to have received the kindness of your mother all these years, let alone enable me to be a proper wife for such a noble man."

A look of hurtful surprise came over Harry's face.

"The differences between our stations in life is all that is holding you back from accepting my true love?" Harry Maylie remarked in frustrated disbelief. "But you do love me as much as I love you?" Harry asked.

Rose was too shy to answer, but the sweet expression in her eyes gave Harry the answer he was seeking.

"Then do not give a final no to my proposal today. Give me time to prove to you that my future includes success, perhaps; but above all, you as my loving wife. Will you grant me that time, my precious Rose?"

"Yes, sweet Harry, yes."

He held her close, kissed her forehead, and left the room.

CHAPTER 14

Important Information

While the summer months progressed so pleasantly for Oliver, they contained quite the opposite sentiments for Mr. Bumble, who very quickly after marrying Mrs. Corney, began to feel regret that he had done so.

He had arranged a transfer to the position of workhouse supervisor, which made it possible for him to wed the widow and become half-owner of her home and household goods. The problem was that he had given up the title and prestige of being an official by marrying Mrs. Corney.

It had not occurred to Mr. Bumble before the marriage ceremony how very much that prestige meant to him. He had traded status and self-esteem for a few worldly possessions, and now the bargain did not seem worth its price.

To make matters even worse, it turned out that the matrimonial match between Mr. Bumble and his new wife was a quarrelsome one. They argued, they fought, they did not get along.

One evening, after yet another fight, Mr. Bumble stormed out of the house and walked hastily to the nearest tavern to find some peace and quiet and a drink.

There was only one other customer in the tavern as Mr. Bumble took a seat across the room. The stranger wore a heavy, black cloak around his head and shoulders. He studied Mr. Bumble several minutes before asking, "Weren't you the official in these parts some years ago?"

"Yes—I am still a government employee—I am supervisor of the workhouse, now." Mr. Bumble puffed up his new title with as much importance as he could muster.

"Um...," replied the stranger. "Does that mean that you would not be interested in making some extra money for the exchange of some information that I might need?"

"On the contrary, I would be very interested."

The cloaked man, with an evil and distrustful manner, then led Mr. Bumble into a conversation about a child born about twelve years previous: a boy named Oliver Twist!

"Yes, I know of the child," Mr. Bumble replied.

The cloaked stranger demanded, "Can you arrange for me to talk with the nurse who attended the baby's mother?"

"I cannot!" Mr. Bumble answered emphatically. "She died six months ago."

Distressed, the stranger inhaled deeply and rose to leave, but Mr. Bumble called him back, for the former official saw a chance to add even more coins to his small purse.

"But I do know in whom the nurse confided just before she died, and I can arrange a meeting with that woman."

"That will do," the stranger hissed, and he quickly scratched an address on a piece of paper and handed it to Mr. Bumble. "Bring her there at 9 p.m. tomorrow."

As the cloaked man turned hastily to leave, Mr. Bumble remembered that there had been no introductions between the two. He called out to the mysterious man, "And whom shall I tell her she is to meet?"

"Monks. Monks, that is all."

Heavy storm clouds gathered and strong gusts of wind pushed against Mr. and Mrs. Bumble the next evening as they looked for the location Monks had indicated on his scrap of paper. The riverside address was that of an abandoned water mill, so rotted now that the whole thing appeared ready to collapse at any time.

Thunder clapped and big raindrops hit their faces just at the moment they saw Monks standing in his doorway. He motioned them inside. Monks wasted no time with small talk, but nervously began, "My question is what did the nurse tell you before she died?"

Mrs. Bumble, being a very shrewd woman, countered, "My question is how much will you pay me for what I heard?"

"What if your information is of no value to me? I must hear it first, then I can know how much to pay."

"No, I will accept twenty-five pounds sterling now, or I will speak nothing."

Exasperated, Monks pushed twenty-five coins across the table to the determined woman just as another peal of thunder filled the room. "Now tell me what happened to the mother of Oliver Twist."

Mrs. Bumble began, "Moments before the young lady died, she placed a ticket in the nurse's hand. She asked Sally to make sure the boy received it, for it would give him dignity."

"The nurse did so?" Monks pressed to move the story on.

"No, Sally held onto the pawnbroker's ticket herself until...until she handed it to me that night six months ago."

Mr. Bumble gasped, for he had not known this fact.

Monks' eyes grew wide as he asked excitedly, "You have the ticket with you now?"

"No." the woman answered.

The man's fury was increasing, so he shouted, "Where is it, then?"

"I turned the ticket in at the pawn shop."

Mrs. Bumble's eyes widened as she reached into her purse for a velvet bag that she passed to the cloaked man and said, "And this is the treasure the pawn broker gave me in exchange!"

Monks opened the bag and found a golden locket engraved with the name, "Agnes," and a date that would have been about one year pre-

Agnes
1831

vious to the child's birth. Inside the locket were two locks of hair and a wedding ring.

"Is that what you wanted?" Mrs. Bumble asked.

"Yes."

"Will it get us into any trouble?"

"No, not anymore, and I'll show you why."

Monks then opened a trap door in the floor below the table. The rushing river could be seen below the opening. The mill had been built with a portion of the building directly over the water.

Monks wrapped the golden locket in its velvet bag and then dropped the bag into the swirling waters. It sank quickly out of sight.

"Our business is now complete. We have all three received what we wanted. Please leave immediately and speak not of this night to anyone."

Thunder cracked, lightning roared, and the river continued on its course.

CHAPTER 15

Nancy's Decision

In the meantime, Sikes had made his way back to his apartment where Nancy continued to attend to his needs. She knew he was an evil man who forced her to commit dishonest deeds, yet he held some attraction for Nancy that made her stay with him.

She followed orders without knowing details of the devious plots. It relieved her conscience not to know too much. But on the night following the Bumble's visit to Monks, Monks made his own visit on Sikes and Fagin. And Nancy overheard a conversation between them that she could not in any way ignore.

She heard the thieves discussing the evil course they had followed against the defenseless Oliver Twist. She was shocked to hear that Monks had known about Oliver from his birth and had been watching Oliver from the shadows for eleven years. He knew where Oliver had spent the summer, and he even knew that on that very day the Maylie household had checked themselves into the Hyde Park Hotel in London since they were on their first day of a holiday. Monks knew the Maylie's planned to set sail in a few days on a short pleasure trip.

Nancy's heart was broken as she learned how the child's true heritage had been hidden from everyone What should she do with this new knowledge that affected Oliver's future so seriously? Nancy considered her options carefully and made some startling decisions. Perhaps because she wanted Oliver to have something she didn't have, namely a future with promise, Nancy made up her mind to do the right thing—and she would do it as soon as Fagin and Monks left the apartment and Sikes was fast asleep.

So, a few hours later, with great determination and much fright, Nancy left the dirty neighborhood of Sikes' apartment and sped block after long block. She finally came to the fashionable hotel in the lovely part of London where the Maylie's were vacationing.

Once inside the apartment and standing face to face with the the lovely Miss Rose, Nancy began to cry.

"Whatever I can do for you, please tell me." Rose's kind heart reached out to anyone in need.

"I ask nothing for me, Miss. It is for poor Oliver Twist that I am here."

"For Oliver! What is it?" Rose urged the girl to go on. Nancy began to tell everything she knew that concerned Oliver's trials and mistreatment including how it was she who had kidnapped Oliver when he was on his way to the Pentonville bookstore.

"What!" cried Rose.

"I know I am a horrible person, Miss, but I have been raised in the dirty alleys of this town without the teachers to show me the right way to live that you, I suspect, have had, Miss."

"I am sorry, my dear," Miss Rose spoke sympathetically, "perhaps I can help you now."

Nancy interrupted, "I must hurry to tell you more, Miss...if I do not return soon, Monks will have me murdered, I am sure."

"Who is Monks?" Miss Rose asked.

"You mean you do not know him?" Nancy responded. "He seems to know you very well. In fact, I was able to find you tonight because I heard Monks tell Sikes and Fagin where you were. Monks is also the one who paid Fagin to turn Oliver into a pickpocket; it is he who threw the locket into the rushing water."

"What locket?"

"The golden locket that belonged to Oliver's mother!" Nancy almost cried as she spoke of the child's parent.

"Why would he do such a thing?" Miss Rose questioned.

"I don't understand all his reasons, Miss, but I did hear him say to Fagin with great anger, 'My brother will never enjoy the advantages of his birth, if I can have my way.'"

"He called Oliver his brother?" gasped Miss Rose.

"Yes, and he also spoke of you...of how much money you would pay to learn the true identity of Oliver Twist!"

"What kind of a cruel person is this Monks? Tell me everything you can...."

"I've said enough tonight, and I must hurry back now."

"You don't mean you intend to rejoin them?"

"I must. They will kill me if they learn I've said anything to you."

"But I'll keep you safe here," Miss Rose pleaded. "Please don't go back into their world."

"It is too late for me to change. My future is hopeless," Nancy whispered.

"No. No. Never give up hope." Miss Rose desperately wanted to offer encouragement to the troubled girl and to rescue her from her life of misery. "We can always choose to turn from our old ways if they are wrong."

But, Nancy turned toward the door, anyway.

"If you go now, what good will it be that you have given me this information? What am I do with this news without you?" Miss Rose spoke pleadingly.

"Surely someone can advise you, Miss, but I must go."

"Where can I find you? It may happen that I will need to speak to you again."

Nancy answered, "On Sunday nights, just before midnight, you can find me walking on the London Bridge. But promise me that if you choose to seek me, you will either come alone or bring only the one person you may ask for advice."

"I do promise."

The two ladies parted, each with a heavy heart—the visitor burdened with regret for all her past sins—Miss Rose deeply troubled that she had not succeeded in convincing Nancy to change her direction and make a new life for herself.

CHAPTER 16

The Kinchin Trade

On this same night, two other characters were also trying to find their way in unfamiliar territory. The reader has met these two before: the young man was tall and thin; the young woman was shorter and stronger. In fact, it was she who carried a heavy bag on her back as this couple walked the northern road into London.

With longer legs and no knapsack to carry, the man's pace was faster than his companion's. Several times he stopped, looked back at the woman, and grumbled, "Keep up with me, Charlotte. Don't be such a lazybones!"

"I am hot and tired, Noah Claypole," the fellow traveler complained as she sat down for a rest along the side of the road. "How much farther is it to London?"

"It doesn't matter how far it is. We've got to keep going or we'll get caught. Now get up or I will kick you!" Noah threatened.

They trudged on, and soon they could see the lights of London. Charlotte demanded, "We are stopping for the night at the first inn we see!"

"Oh, no, we're not!" countered Noah. "Don't you think that will be the first place Sowerberry looks for us if he decides to track us to London? It's a good thing I'm doing the thinking for us, Charlotte, because if I hadn't thought of going cross-country instead of the regular path, you would be locked up right now for taking the money."

"I took the money for you, Noah," Charlotte snapped.

"Yes, but I've let you hold on to it, haven't I?" Noah continued.

Charlotte took Noah's action as a compliment without realizing the true reason her selfish companion had given her such trust. It was so that the stolen money would be found in her bag if they got caught and then he'd say he had known nothing of it.

They entered the gates of London, and Noah looked for an inn far away from the main road. He found a place called The Three Cripples and checked Charlotte and himself in for the night, stopping first in the dining area for a supper of roast beef.

A few minutes later, Fagin stopped by, for the Three Cripples was a meeting place for several of his boys. His friend, the innkeeper, motioned for Fagin to take note of the two new travelers having supper at the far table.

"I think they are robbers, Fagin, don't you?"

The scruffy-looking Noah and tattered Charlotte were, indeed, just the sort that held Fagin's interest. He nonchalantly took a seat at a table close enough to hear their conversation, but around the corner out of their view.

"We are going to have the rich city life, now Charlotte, just you wait and see," Fagin heard Noah say to the girl.

"But how?" Charlotte asked. "All we know to do is pick the pockets of dead people before Sowerberry makes their coffins. It hasn't made us rich."

"I know, Charlotte, but in the city there's much more opportunity for grabbing after bigger stakes, and there are people who will teach you how," Noah gloated with his worldly knowledge.

"What we need is someone to teach us how to get rid of that marked twenty-note in my bag. You know it will be traced to us if we spend it," Charlotte spoke with worried tones.

This part of the conversation was all Fagin needed to hear to stir his appetite for more accomplices to ensnare in his traps of vice. He moved to an even closer table and exchanged a few pleasantries with the newcomers. "Traveling from the country, I see," Fagin observed to the couple.

"How do you figure that?" Noah questioned.

"Oh, by the dust on your boots and the knapsack at your feet," Fagin answered.

"You are a pretty smart fellow," said Noah.

"And thirsty, too," Fagin added, as he called to the innkeeper for a special kind of bottle to be brought to the travelers' table, and he invited himself to sit down with them.

"Whew! This is expensive stuff," remarked Noah as he drained the glass Fagin poured for him.

"Yes, much too costly for one who robs coffins, I would say," Fagin added slyly.

Noah swallowed hard and stammered, "She took it, not me. It was her doing, not mine." Noah's back stiffened in fear.

"Then I tip my hat in admiration to the young lady," Fagin grinned, "since she and I follow the same trade...as do most of the customers of this inn's business. This is our safe place."

Fagin turned to Noah, "And I can get you into the trade, if you are interested. All I have to do is introduce you to the head man."

"How much would it cost me?" Noah replied.

"A twenty-note would do nicely," Fagin commented, letting Noah and Charlotte know how much he already could accuse them of if they were to say they wanted no part of his business.

"What can you teach me?" Noah asked. "I don't want to start with anything too dangerous."

Fagin thought the matter over and answered, "I would say, then, that the kinchin jobs are made for you."

"What are 'kinchin' jobs?" Noah wondered.

"That is what we call London's young children who run errands for their parents and carry sixpence in their hands. All people like us have to do is knock the tykes down and grab their coins. It's that easy. The crowded city is full of the little kinchins!"

"I guess I can do 'kinchins,' then." Noah twisted his face to say the strange word, and they all three had a good laugh.

And so the next day, Fagin took Noah and Charlotte to his apartment. He introduced

them to Charley Bates and began instructing the newcomers in the troubling side of the crime business such as how to avoid the hangman's gallows! His mood was much darker than it had been the night before, and Noah did not like it.

"The gallows!" Noah shouted. "Why do you speak of such horrors?"

"Because I have seen enough scoundrels just like me who have come to an untimely end because they were not careful enough. I have experienced enough to know that we must always look out after each other," Fagin spoke in great earnestness. He added, "Your safety is my number one concern, and my safety is your number one priority, or we will all hang together, do you understand?"

Noah nodded.

Fagin's voice kept on trembling as he said further, "I am already in great danger this morning...they got one of my best boys last night."

"Why?" Noah asked.

"How?" asked Charlotte.

"The police," Fagin roared, "they got the Dodger for pickpocketing. He was the best thief I've ever had...oh, if I could only get some word to him."

"I'll sneak into his jail cell," Charley offered. "I want to see him as badly as you do...I still can't believe they got the Dodger." Charley's voice was incredulous, for he was nearly in shock.

"I will not let you go!" Fagin shouted. "I could not bear to lose you both."

"But someone must find out what the Dodger's up against," Charley wailed. "If you won't send me, then send him." Charley nodded toward Noah.

Fagin saw the merit in this idea, since Noah was as yet under no suspicions of crimes committed in London. He charged Noah with the duty of dressing in disguise and going to the courtroom to hear word about the once "artful" Dodger who, this time, had not dodged the police.

Thus, attired in leather trousers, a home-spun shirt, and a velvet vest, Noah looked like a man who, on his way to market, had stopped for a moment to attend the day's court proceedings.

He mingled his way into the crowd and listened to several cases before he saw a suspect he decided must be the Dodger. It was the pickpocket's cocky way in which he walked to the defendant's chair and his air of indifference that convinced Noah this must be the fellow Fagin had described.

Noah heard the judge ask, "Who are the witnesses against this boy?"

"I will speak first, your honor," a policeman answered. "I saw this young man pick a handkerchief from the pocket of a man in the crowd yesterday. And when I nabbed the boy, I searched his pockets and also found this silver key ring. I brought the ruffian into jail, sir,

and consulted the list of complaints we had received of stolen property. On that list was this exact silver key ring, for it is engraved with the owner's initials. I called in the person reporting the key ring stolen, and he is here ready to testify also."

The judge looked at the man indicated, and he asked, "Is this your silver key ring, and was it stolen from you?"

"It is, your honor; and yes, it was taken from me yesterday morning."

The Artful Dodger was questioned next, but he had no defense, so he was convicted and led away to jail.

CHAPTER 17

Incredible Turns

By this time, Miss Rose had only two days to solve the mystery of Oliver's plight before they set sail. Over and over in her mind that evening, she pondered her dilemma: to whom could she turn for advice?

Miss Rose gratefully noted how the good Dr. Losberne had suggested the right course of action when Oliver had first come to them. But now that the doctor was so attached to the boy, she wondered if his anger would be riled excessively and if he would do something quickly—before thinking it through—which would put dear Nancy in danger.

Was Mrs. Maylie the right person to ask for advice? Miss Rose asked herself. *No,* the young lady decided, *for Mrs. Maylie would call in Dr. Losberne.*

Could it be that Harry could help...and if he could, do I have the courage to ask for his assistance? Miss Rose then pondered.

All night she tossed and turned in perplexity. The next morning, Miss Rose's mind was still going over and over the incredible tale Nancy had brought her, when Oliver ran breathlessly into her room with an incredible tale of his own.

"We saw him, we saw him," Oliver exclaimed. "He is right here in London."

"Who's here? What are you saying? Slow down, Oliver, and tell me your news."

"We saw Mr. Brownlow!" Oliver explained. "Giles and I were out for an early morning walk, and we saw good Mr. Brownlow!"

"Where was he? Did you speak to him?"

"We saw him entering a house on Craven Street...and no, I was too frightened to call after him. But I must see him...oh, Miss Rose, I am overjoyed! Do you think it is possible that I can see him?"

"I shall take you there myself!" Miss Rose answered speedily, "Ask Giles to call us a coach."

A few minutes later, their coach drew up to the Craven Street address. Miss Rose instructed Oliver to wait there until she had been properly introduced to good Mr. Brownlow.

Miss Rose spoke to the servant who answered the door and said she had very important business with Mr. Brownlow.

The servant led Miss Rose to the upstairs sitting room where Mr. Brownlow was having tea with his friend, Mr. Grimwig.

Thus, Miss Rose met the kind gentleman and his unusual friend and said to them, "It must seem very surprising for a stranger such

as myself to ask for this unscheduled audience with you." Miss Rose began very shyly, "But I am certain you will want to hear what I can tell you about a lad named Oliver Twist."

"Oliver Twist!" cried Mr. Brownlow, who was, indeed, surprised. "I pray you have brought evidence that the boy is the sweet child I first thought him to be."

Eagerly, Miss Rose told Mr. Brownlow all she knew of Oliver's story, emphasizing how desirous the boy had been all these many months to clear his reputation with the good gentleman.

Mr. Brownlow's face gleamed with anticipation, he sat on the edge of his chair and spoke, "The only thing that could make me happier than I am at hearing these words would be seeing the child again—where is he, young lady?"

"He is downstairs in the coach, he...."

Mr. Brownlow did not wait for Miss Rose to finish her sentence. He rushed to the coach immediately.

The joy the young man and the old gentleman experienced when at last their eyes met could only be matched by the thrill in Mrs. Bedwin's heart when, as Mr. Brownlow led Oliver into the dwelling, the housekeeper came running to the entrance and welcomed Oliver with open arms.

"Let me look at you, child!" Mrs. Bedwin wept. "Every day since you left, I have kept your face in my memory, and now you are here in person!"

Mrs. Bedwin tossled the boy's wavy, chestnut hair and hugged him several times.

The two gentlemen, the two ladies, and Oliver went to the sitting room and chatted joyously as the kitchen servant carried in a tray of festive cakes to add to the tea service. It was a happy time of celebration!

A half hour later, while Oliver, Mr. Grimwig, and the housekeeper continued conversing, Miss Rose drew Mr. Brownlow aside and confided in him Nancy's addition to the story of Oliver Twist.

"How can we resolve this situation, Mr. Brownlow?" Miss Rose asked for the gentleman's advice.

They decided that Mr. Brownlow would confide the facts to Dr. Losberne being careful not to arouse any sudden reactions from the man, and Miss Rose would speak to Mrs. Maylie. Then, the four would meet at the hotel that evening at 8 p.m. to agree on a plan of action.

As suspected, when Mr. Brownlow communicated the entire account to the doctor early that evening, Dr. Losberne's anger was kindled unmercifully upon all the culprits in Oliver's story. Impulsively, he would have collected the whole brood of robbers and punished them himself if he had not been restrained by the better reasoning of Mr. Brownlow, who was very upset as well.

Their anger was under better control that evening, however, when they met with the ladies. Yet it was still with much exasperation that the doctor asked Mr. Brownlow, "Exactly how do you propose we bring these criminals to justice?"

"Perhaps, even before justice is applied, there is another goal that must be achieved," the gentleman added.

"What is that, sir?" Mrs. Maylie asked.

"We must learn the names of Oliver's parents so that we can restore his inheritance."

"You have a plan how their names can be discovered?" the doctor asked.

"Yes. Monks is the key, of course," Mr. Brownlow replied. "We must find him and speak to him alone. In order to do so, we must have that young lady, Nancy, tell us where he is."

"Nancy cannot be contacted until Sunday night—that is five more days," Miss Rose reminded them.

"Enough time for us to calculate our plans precisely. That is if you, Mrs. Maylie, do not mind postponing your trip until this matter can be resolved."

"Of course I do not mind," Mrs. Maylie said. "We will remain in London as long as necessary."

"Now, let me say," Mr. Brownlow added, "that if this plan works as I hope it will, there shall come a time when I can add a few pieces to this puzzle—pieces that I must hold in confidence now so as not to get your hopes up too high. I ask for your patience with me; but for my own sake, I shall be relieved when I can fully explain to you my reasons for leaving the country so suddenly when Oliver came up missing."

Then, Mr. Brownlow continued, "And to help with the plan, I suggest we bring my friend, Mr. Grimwig, into our confidence. He is a retired lawyer, and his expertise will be of great value. Does anyone object?" Mr. Brownlow questioned Miss Rose, Mrs. Maylie, and Dr. Losberne.

The doctor answered for all three, "No objection, sir, and may I also suggest a friend?"

"Whom might that be, good doctor?" Mr. Brownlow asked.

Dr. Losberne answered, "Harry Maylie, sir. Mrs. Maylie's son and Miss Rose's...ah... friend."

Miss Rose blushed but nodded yes. Mrs. Maylie and Mr. Brownlow both agreed.

CHAPTER 18

Just a Little Walk

As the days progressed, Nancy was in great distress. It had been hard to reveal the greedy business her associates had devised against Oliver, but she knew it had been the right thing to do. She was comforted, though, by the fact that she had protected Bill Sikes' name as much as she could.

Still, she must keep her secret from Sikes and all the others. If they found out about the information she had given Miss Rose, Sikes would horse whip her…or worse—thus, she could not calm her nerves.

Finally it was Sunday night. Fagin and Sikes were at the supper table while Nancy was washing up the dishes, when at last she heard a church bell strike 11 p.m. Nancy gathered her bonnet and shawl and prepared to leave the house when Sikes noticed her plans and yelled, "Where are you going?"

"For a little walk," Nancy replied.

"Where?"

"Just a little walk," she repeated.

"You are not answering my question...and until you do, you will stay right here," Sikes shouted as he pulled her back, tore off her bonnet, and locked the outside door.

"No, I'm not!" Nancy screamed and stamped her feet as if in a temper tantrum.

"I think you have lost your mind!" Sikes snarled as he grabbed both of Nancy's arms and shook her violently.

They fought for several minutes until Nancy was out of strength and Sikes pushed her into a chair where she sat sobbing until she heard the clock strike midnight. Then her body went limp, and she sighed in desperation, for it was too late to meet Miss Rose if the good lady had chosen to come to London Bridge that night.

Sikes led her to the bedroom, then returned to the kitchen and spoke with annoyance to Fagin, "I don't know what's come over the girl!"

"Umm...stubbornness, I guess," Fagin suggested.

"Or maybe she caught that wretched fever I suffered from last week," Sikes muttered.

"Maybe," Fagin said aloud, but to himself he pondered another explanation that seemed much more plausible to him but which he would never reveal to Sikes.

Then, although frazzled from tears and her struggles with Sikes, Nancy suddenly appeared in the kitchen. She sat at the table and started to laugh at nothing in particular.

Her odd behavior was about all Sikes could take, and he looked at Fagin in disbelief.

Fagin shrugged his shoulders and decided it was time to leave. "Will one of you light my way down the stairs?" he asked.

Sikes ordered the girl, "Nancy, get a candle and light his way."

Nancy did so; and when she and Fagin reached the last step outside, Fagin found the opportunity he wanted. He whispered to Nancy, "What is going on? What is making you so frantic? You know you can come to me at any time, if he is mistreating you. You do know that, don't you, Nancy?"

"Yes."

"And you will come?" he pressed for further reply. Nancy did not answer, but the two exchanged knowing glances that seemed to satisfy Fagin for the time being. They said good night.

As Fagin walked to his apartment, he mulled over the strange scene he had witnessed during the last hour, and he came to his own conclusions. *She must have found*

another man who has captured her affections, Fagin thought to himself.

And since Fagin had never relished working with the rather vicious Bill Sikes, he decided he might help Nancy run away and attach herself to whomever this new man might be. *It would serve Sikes right*, Fagin mused.

However, the more he thought of Sikes' intense meanness, the clearer it was to Fagin that Nancy would never survive an attempt to

run away. *No, Sikes would find her and force her to come back*, Fagin realized.

Fagin considered how much he himself hated the ruthless man, and he said his thoughts aloud to himself, "The only chance for Nancy to be free of him is if he is dead. With Sikes gone, Nancy will be completely under my control." Fagin then determined that all this could be achieved if he could convince Nancy to drop some poison into Sikes' bowl of soup!

Fagin was delighted with his evil imaginations. His thoughts raced on until they stopped abruptly with the question of how he could possibly talk Nancy into poisoning Sikes.

"She will do it if," Fagin finally decided, "I find out who this new man is in her affections, and I threaten her with telling Sikes about him."

With every step Fagin took, therefore, the plot in his head became more devious and proved without doubt that his motives were not in helping Nancy, but in removing a man whom he hated with a passion.

By the next morning, Fagin had completed his plans, so he waited anxiously for Noah Claypole, who would have a part in the plot. Finally, the boy arrived at Fagin's apartment and sat down at the breakfast table.

"Your first day in the kinchin trade was very fruitful, Noah. Six shillings is a good take. I will just keep my half and here are three shillings for you," Fagin expressed much satisfaction with his newest pupil.

Noah took the shillings and also grabbed another large slice of toasted bread and devoured it greedily while Fagin talked on.

"I think you are ready for a more elevated assignment," Fagin continued.

"Nothing dangerous," Noah reminded the man between mouthfuls.

"No, this isn't dangerous," Fagin assured him. "I want you to follow someone and tell me all the places the person goes."

"How much will you pay me?" Noah wanted to know.

"My highest wage for a job like this: one pound sterling silver."

"Who is it?"

"One of my own, Noah," the old man replied.

"Ah...one who has crossed you?" the boy wondered aloud.

"No, but one who may have found some new friends that I would like to know about."

"It's a deal," Noah responded. "Now tell me the details."

Fagin explained that he wanted to know the activities of a young woman named Nancy. Noah was to spy on the girl in order to report to the old man all the places she visited and all the people she met.

So it was that on the following Sunday night, as Nancy nervously set out on her midnight mission, Noah Claypole was trailing along behind, hiding in the shadows, never losing sight of the girl who walked with cautious determination to London Bridge.

Chapter 19

On London Bridge

The clock bell tower struck 11:45 as Nancy, who thought she was alone, and Noah, who cautiously followed her, approached the London Bridge. Noah stayed far enough away not to arouse Nancy's suspicions, but close enough not to lose her.

Twelve chimes rang from the clock tower to announce the midnight hour. A carriage stopped at the entrance of the bridge and two passengers stepped out: an older gentleman with gray hair and a young lady in silken bonnet and cape. As soon as Nancy saw the two, she ran to them—and Noah followed several paces behind.

Nancy led the couple down cold, dark steps, which brought them to a lonely landing closer to the shore line. Noah found a place to hide on one side of a huge column that supported the bridge.

"Why have you brought us to such a dark and treacherous place?" Mr. Brownlow used a voice that was not kind. "I will not have the lady slip and come to any harm."

"Harm the lady! It is I who is in great danger," Nancy's voice trembled. "I have been out of my head with fear the entire day."

"I am sorry," the gentleman regathered his sympathy. "What is frightening you the most, my dear?"

"Death," Nancy answered solemnly. "I have felt all day that I shall meet my death before tomorrow dawns."

"Nonsense," the gentleman responded. "It has only been your imagination."

The lady in the bonnet saw the terror in Nancy's eyes and said to the gentleman,

"Give her nothing but kindness, sir. She needs compassion."

"You are right, Miss Rose," Mr. Brownlow agreed. He used warmer tones to ask Nancy, "We waited for you here last Sunday, child. Why did you not come?"

"The man, in whose house I stay, prevented me from leaving."

"Does he know you have left the house tonight?" Miss Rose asked the girl.

"No, he has no suspicions tonight. He has gone out on a job of his own and does not know that I have left the house."

"Then let us proceed," the gentleman continued. "Miss Rose has confided in me the information you gave her, and we are asking that you let us know how to find the man called Monks... And, if we cannot locate Monks, you must tell us how to get to Fagin."

"Fagin!" Nancy exclaimed. "No, I will never turn on Fagin."

"But why?" Miss Rose spoke softly.

"I explained before, Miss. I know he has led me—and many others—into crime but we have always protected one another. It is the only protection I have ever known. I will not turn on any of them."

Miss Rose and Mr. Brownlow were distressed that Nancy would not give up the gang entirely, but there seemed no way to convince her otherwise. Nancy spoke again, "You will

not tell Monks that it was I who helped you find him?"

"We will not tell him," the gentleman answered firmly.

Nancy responded, "Because I am a liar and have lived with liars all my life, I believe almost no one. But your promise, I will trust."

So, Nancy revealed her secret information to the couple. She spoke so quietly that Noah had to strain his ears to hear. Noah listened to Nancy's account of Monks' conversation with Fagin in which Monks had said, "The proof of the boy's heritage now lies buried beneath the muddy, river waters."

Noah made mental notes of Nancy's information while Mr. Brownlow took notes on a small tablet. Nancy furnished a description of the man called Monks, directions to the Three Cripples Inn, and a schedule of times that he usually visited it. Noah heard Nancy say, "He is a young man, probably not thirty yet, but his worried countenance makes him look much older. His lips and hands often show teeth marks from moments when he has bit himself in violent fits."

"Oh no!" the gentleman responded before he could hold his tongue.

Nancy's voice came to a startled stop.

Mr. Brownlow quickly tried to conceal his distress and asked the girl to go on.

"He wears a large, black cloak around his face," Nancy continued, "and a scarf around his neck so that you cannot see...." Nancy hesitated again as she once more saw a look of recognition fill the eyes of Mr. Brownlow.

The discouraged gentleman then finished her sentence for her, "...so that you cannot see a large, red scald mark on his neck."

"You know who he is!" Nancy gasped in shocked surprise.

"Perhaps, I do," answered the gentleman. Then, so as not to alarm the women any further, he added, "But, perhaps several men would fit the same description."

Mr. Brownlow cleared his throat, "Now, you have given us all the help we need," he concluded, "except to tell us whatever we can do for you in return."

"There is nothing," Nancy answered simply.

"Please, young woman," the gentleman begged. "We cannot clear your conscience for the life you have led so far—only you can do that with your Creator—but we do have the means to send you to any place of safety in the world that you might choose. You can make new friends and never associate with your evil companions again. Please let us do this for you."

"No," Nancy said again. "I feel the chains of death tightening upon me; it is too late for me to change."

"We must let her go," Mr. Brownlow reluctantly conceded to Miss Rose. "We may even have endangered her by keeping her this long."

"Yes, I must go," Nancy said hastily and started to depart.

"Wait, please," Miss Rose called her back. "Accept this purse of money for a little security in case you need it someday."

"I will take no money," Nancy spoke firmly. Then her voice softened, "But I would cherish some small item that has belonged to you. Perhaps a glove...or a handkerchief."

Nancy then accepted the small gift that Miss Rose placed in her hand and responded, "Thank you, Miss Rose, thank you. Now leave me to my course."

Miss Rose and Mr. Brownlow walked slowly up the stairs to the waiting coach. As soon as Nancy watched the carriage ride away, she collapsed on the cold stone stairs. She sat on the step and sobbed anguished tears until she could collect her strength to stumble home.

A few hours later, still in the deepest night when almost no one is about, Fagin sat frozen in rage and watched the flames of his fireplace crackle upon the hearth.

He had been sitting there not moving for the past two hours, ever since Noah Claypole had returned and reported all he had seen and heard on London Bridge.

Fagin's black heart and evil mind twisted and turned the account of the night's meeting. He hated Nancy for betraying them, he regretted the loss of his plan to be rid of Sikes, and he feared for his own discovery.

A knock came on his door, for Sikes was reporting in with his night's booty. The robber entered, placed his bundle on the table and saw with fright the rage that filled the old man's eyes.

"What is it?" Sikes demanded. "You look as if you have lost your mind!"

"As you will, also, when I tell you what I know," Fagin spoke through clenched teeth.

"Sit down," Fagin ordered, "and listen until I am through."

He began, "Suppose I were to tell you that one of my boys had voluntarily—for no reason of obtaining his own escape, just by his own devices—met with people and had told them all our plots, described every one of us to them and even given directions to all the locations where we could be found. What would you do to the boy, Sikes?" Fagin demanded.

"I would crush his skull," Sikes snarled.

"Suppose I was the person who turned traitor, Sikes. What then?"

"I would blow your head off," Sikes' anger flared, and he reached for the pistol in his pocket, "as I would do to anyone who tried to turn me in."

"Even Nancy?" Fagin roared, "For it is she I speak of."

"What!"

Sikes was outraged and paced the floor as Fagin repeated all that Noah had said. Every word fed Sikes' wrath until he cursed and stormed toward the door.

"Bill!" Fagin shouted after him, "Don't be so violent that...." He stopped and looked at Sikes with the same anger he saw flaming in Sikes' pupils. They both knew what Sikes planned to do, and Fagin joined the deed by adding, "Don't be so violent that we will be caught."

Bill Sikes tore through the streets to his apartment, he rushed into the bedroom and awakened the girl, who was asleep in her bed. She had thought herself now to be in no danger.

Circling his hands around her neck and shaking her severely, he pulled her out of bed.

"What is it, Bill?" Nancy screamed, still not sensing that it was possible that the violent man had learned of her midnight walk.

"I know all about your sneaking tales, Miss Nancy, and the whole story you spilled to two strangers on London Bridge tonight."

"Bill, I did not use your name. Bill, I would never do that...and the gentleman said he

could send me to a place of safety anywhere. We can both go, Bill, you and me. We can start over again clean somewhere. Please, Bill, hear me," Nancy pleaded.

"I will not. I am finished with you!"

The outraged man pulled the pistol from his pocket and used the end of the gun to slam the girl's head once and then again until a gaping wound gushed blood down her face.

Nancy fell to her knees. With her last strength, she pulled the lace handkerchief—Miss Rose's gift to her—from her pocket and raised it toward Heaven in a prayer for forgiveness. Bill Sikes showed no mercy. He stood aside as the wounded girl fell to the floor and breathed her last.

CHAPTER 20

On the Run

A gorgeous, golden daybreak came to London the next morning. The sunlight filtered through every window—from the stained glass windows of cathedrals to the shabby, cracked windows of Bill Sikes' apartment.

The murderer had not moved for hours. When the morning light broke through the curtains and showed plainly what he had done, he trembled. He washed the blood off his hands and arms, but still the girl's body lay lifeless on the floor. He could stand to be in the room no longer, so he carefully stepped out of the apartment, locked the door, and walked away.

But where could he go? There was nowhere in the city to hide for long. So, he walked to the open fields north of town, slept a short while under a tree, and awoke only to wander the countryside some more.

He neared a village tavern and wanted to buy food and drink, but he imagined all the people standing idly outside the inn—even the children—looked at him suspiciously as if they knew what he had done. Though he was hungry and thirsty, he could not take the risk of being noticed, so he rambled on down the road. Finally, as the shadows of evening made him feel safer, he turned into another country inn, sat at a corner table, and ate a few bites of supper.

The strain, the tension, and his weariness made Sikes drowsy and he was about to fall asleep at the inn table when a traveling peddler entered the room. The brightly clothed man carried all of his merchandise in a knapsack, and he had a little bit of everything to sell to anyone.

Even better, the traveling salesman sang an amusing sales pitch and entertained the crowds with jolly, spirited, and exaggerated descriptions of the qualities, benefits, and amazing uses of his many products. He held the attention of everyone in the room.

"You take this potion, for instance, my friends," the winsome man began, "and you can remove any stain there is from any fabric you can name."

He continued, "Does anyone have anything I can test it on?"

When no one offered anything for the demonstration, the salesman looked across the room for shirts with grease stains or towels with wine stains. He saw a blot on the felt hat of Mr. Bill Sikes.

By the time Sikes realized what was happening, the peddler had ambled over to the murderer's chair. "Here, this stain will do," the jolly man sang as he snatched Sikes' hat off his head and announced to the crowd, "you see this spot here? I don't know what it is, it may be a cherry stain, it may be a...blood stain...."

The peddler's sing-song faltered, and Sikes, who had lunged from the table in a flash, angrily yanked the hat from the salesman's hand. Sikes threw a few coins on the table to pay his bill and then fled into the night.

Once again, he was on the run, but the weight of his guilty conscience was increasing. As he ran through the woods, every tree silhouetted in the moonlight appeared to be the spirit of young Nancy chasing him. He could not get away from the frightening sights, for no murderer escapes punishment for long. Everywhere he turned, he saw the still, cold eyes of Nancy. He could find no peace.

Then, suddenly, even the quiet of the night was broken by loud noises and many shouts in the distance. He looked around and saw the red glow of a huge fire across the field.

"No one will notice me with all that confusion," Sikes said to himself. "They won't remember who's there and who's not."

Sikes ran toward the blaze as did villagers from every corner. A farmhouse and its stables were on fire, and everyone wanted to help if they could.

Even Sikes lost himself in the crowd of fire-fighters. He passed buckets of water, he kicked out burning embers, he took risks that no other would take, for fighting the ferocious fire was less frightening than extinguishing the shadows he had confronted in the woods.

But, alas, the good neighbors and the fire station crew from London finally stomped out the last flickering flame, and Sikes' internal terror returned. He turned to walk into the woods once more, but a few of the villagers called him back to offer him a drink.

Not wanting to arouse any suspicions by refusing, Sikes paused for a drink and listened to their conversations. The firemen from London talked about a dreadful murder of a young woman the previous evening in a rundown neighborhood in the north part of the city.

Sikes did not stay to hear any more. He retreated into the woods as quickly as he could.

CHAPTER 21

A Story to Tell

If it had been a strange sight to see Bill Sikes, a murderer on the run, joining a crew fighting to save a neighbor's property, it was an equally strange sight to see a man, with his hands tied behind his back, entering Mr. Brownlow's apartment.

Mr. Brownlow and two of his friends had overtaken the illusive man called Monks as he left the Three Cripples Inn that evening, and now they were leading him into the study at Mr. Brownlow's home. Determined that he would learn the truth from him this night, Mr. Brownlow ordered Monks to sit and answer his questions.

"Why are you doing this to me?" Monks snarled.

"Whatever consequences come to you, Monks, you have brought them on yourself," Mr. Brownlow answered.

"And is this a proper way for my father's best friend to treat me?" the cloaked man sneered.

"It is only because he was my dearest friend and his sister my loving fiance…it is only because we comforted each other in our grief when she died on the day that was to be our wedding celebration…it is only because I stood beside him through his life's trials until his death…and it is only because I see his resemblance in you, Edward Leeford, that I have not turned you over to the authorities but have first given you this chance to explain yourself."

"And what do you want me to explain?"

"Tell me about your brother."

"There is no brother. I was an only child, as you very well know," Monks snapped.

"Yes, I know the story of how your grandfather forced my friend to marry a woman he did not love to secure a rich estate for the Leeford family. I watched that ill-fated marriage rot from the very start until there was nothing but hatred between the husband and wife...until they couldn't stand the sight of each other."

"Yes, and they separated," Monks sneered.

"Years passed, Monks," Mr. Brownlow continued. "Your mother forgot she even had a husband. And then your father met a lovely young lady, the daughter of a retired naval officer named Captain Fleming. She was sweet and beautiful. They became good friends and then they fell in love. It was the first real love my friend had ever received, but how I wish it had ended there."

"But it didn't," snarled Monks, "did it?"

"No. No, for my friend was determined to marry the young woman even though he was still legally bound to your mother. He visited me one afternoon to ask my advice and help with the paperwork. He was on his way to a short stay in Paris to visit a sick relative, but as soon as he returned to England, he planned to file for divorce. He made generous financial

arrangements for you and your mother and as a gift for me, he brought a portrait that he had painted himself. It was a picture of a lovely lady...his beloved. However, as you know, he never returned from Paris, but caught a fever while visiting there and died."

Mr. Brownlow halted for a moment, respectful of his friend's memory, and then continued. "I tried to find the young woman to help her if I could, but her family had suddenly packed up their things and moved to an unknown location."

The gentleman continued, "Therefore, I was left without my best friend and without any way of helping his reputation until years later, when I saw a young child whom, I believe, God placed in my way. Then, this young child, whose face brought back whispers of memories to me...was snatched away before I fully realized who he was. Ah, but Monks, that part you know."

"Why would I know it?" Monks asked.

"Don't act as if you know nothing. I know differently. I was so sure that you were involved in the crafty plot, I even set sail for the West Indies to search for you, for I had heard you had last been seen there. And, when I couldn't find you there, I returned to London and have scoured the streets for you ever since."

"Why? Because you think I have a brother! Because you think I have done him harm! You have no proof that I have cheated him. You don't even know for sure if my father and this young woman had a child!" Monks' voice was surly.

"Yes, I do, as do you. Just as you told Fagin that 'the proof of the boy's heritage now lies buried beneath the muddy, river waters.' You see, I know that your father had left a will that mentioned this second child. I know that your mother destroyed this will but not before telling you of your half brother. I know that you found the boy and have hounded him all his life. You—his father's firstborn—who is a partner with thieves and murderers!"

"I have committed no murder!" Monks cried. "I heard of Nancy's death just this morning and was going to learn the consequences of what I thought had been an argument between her and her killer when your men kidnapped me in the streets!"

"It was, indeed, an argument," Mr. Brownlow interjected, "and it dealt with a partial history of your involvement with young Oliver. Now it is time for you to tell me the rest. Are you ready to reveal the entire story or shall I go to the police with what I can imagine are the remaining facts?"

Monks took a very deep breath. Reluctantly he gave in and said, "If you put it that way, I am ready."

"And will you allow me to put your statement in writing so that you may sign it as document-proof of the truth? And will you return to the boy the part of the inheritance that belongs to him?"

Monks jumped to his feet in anger. He paced the floor agitatedly and tried to calculate the chances of his getting away without agreeing to this last proposal. Suddenly Dr. Losberne unlocked the door and stormed in with the news that the murderer's trail was unraveling. "They have found Bill Sikes' dog,

and the mutt is circling a rundown hideaway on Jacob's Island. Either Sikes is inside or he will be coming there. It won't be long before he is caught!"

"And where is Harry?" questioned Mr. Brownlow.

"He is riding his horse with the search party."

"Has anyone nabbed Fagin yet?" Mr. Brownlow was hungry for news.

"Not yet, but the rumor is he will be behind bars within hours," Dr. Losberne replied.

Turning to Monks, Mr. Brownlow asked again, "Have you made your decision?"

Monks was smart enough to understand that time was running out. He had better make the best arrangements he could before an angry posse on horseback came after him, too. He curled his lip in disgust, but otherwise showed no emotion. He looked Mr. Brownlow straight in the eyes and answered, "Yes, I will do as you say."

CHAPTER 22

No Escape

The dirtiest, lowliest section of London was an area along the Thames River called Jacob's Island. It was made up of muddy, narrow alleys that snaked between abandoned buildings where bricks fell from crumbling chimneys and door hinges rusted away. It was not a place fit for human habitat, and if anyone did set up a temporary home here, it was only because he was either totally penniless or hiding from the law.

On this particular afternoon, in an upstairs room of one of these buildings, there sat two robbers. The one was named Toby Crackit and the other called Kags. They sat in silence. The

day's tumultuous events were jumbled in their minds.

Finally, Toby spoke, "When did they get Fagin?"

"About 2 p.m. The three of us boys hustled out the back door of his apartment when we heard the police coming. Charley Bates and I ran and hid under the front porch, but Noah crawled headfirst into an empty rain barrel. His legs were too long to pull all the way in, though, and the coppers nailed him," Kags explained.

"And where is Charley now?" Toby asked.

"For some reason, he wanted to lag behind. I don't know why or where he is going. I expect he will turn up here tonight. He can't hide out at the Three Cripples because the police have got the whole gang in jail, and the place is being watched by undercover detectives."

"This is the end, isn't it? We are all going to be stopped, aren't we?" Toby asked and spoke with a voice that sounded as if he couldn't believe what he had just said.

"I would say so," Kags answered. "As soon as Noah testifies to save his own skin, I'm sure he will turn in the evidence against Fagin. Fagin will hang by this weekend, I'd say."

"You should have seen how the crowd fought Fagin as the police tried to pull him away through the streets," Kags added. "Me and Charley watched the whole thing from between the broken slats in the porch. They dragged him along, and the mob was pressing in, punching him, scratching him, swearing that they would see him hang."

Just then, Toby and Kags heard the clip-clop sound of a small animal coming up the stairs to their second-story room.

"What's that?" whispered Kags.

"It's Sikes' dog!" Toby Crackit fearfully exclaimed.

"Oh, no! Is he here?" Kags screamed.

The two robbers ran to every window but saw no sight of the man whose name they could not bring themselves to say.

After a few minutes of search, Toby replied, "I think the dog is alone. We can relax."

Quietly, they gave the animal some water to drink, for he was panting from exhaustion. Then, they settled into a hushed conversation of the day's events until the afternoon faded into evening.

Suddenly, the two robbers stopped their talking, because they heard a rapid knocking on the door.

"He wouldn't knock, so maybe it's Charley," Kags whispered.

"No, that's not Charley's knock," Toby cautioned as he looked out a broken window to the first-story entrance below. "It is him, and we have to let the wretch in, or he will shoot us on the spot."

"I know," admitted Kags, "let him in."

So, Mr. Bill Sikes came in without saying a word. His haunted eyes were sunken in his face. Three days' worth of whiskers covered his taut, strained face.

The dusk deepened and the robbers lit a couple candles, but they tried not to look at the murderer. And when he asked if Fagin was caught, they didn't even answer.

Sikes cursed them and then yelled at Toby, "Are you going to let me stay the night here or not!"

"I guess," Toby replied.

A few more minutes of nervous silence passed, then Sikes growled, "Is she buried?"

"No, not yet," Kags answered.

"What! Why not!" Sikes shrieked and jumped as another knock came on the door.

"It must be Charley," Toby said as he went downstairs to let the young pickpocket in.

So, Charley Bates followed Toby upstairs not realizing the murderer was up there, too.

When Charley saw Sikes, he screamed, "You monster! I hate you, I hate you."

Charley clenched his fists to tear into Sikes, but Toby and Kags held him back.

Charley struggled with them and cried, "Help me take him. Even if it kills me, I'll rip him apart."

At this remark, Charley pulled free of his companions and toppled Sikes to the floor. They wrestled and punched each other until Toby and Kags heard a commotion outside, and they pulled the two fighters apart.

The noise and confusion were coming from the huge crowd of angry, screaming citizens who had run toward the broken-down house. They lined the muddy shoreline and filled every inch of the bridge attached to Jacob's Island. They knew Sikes was cornered, and they were not going to let him get away.

In the middle of the mob was a man on horseback, who, seeing the candlelight in the

upper window, yelled, "He's got to be on the second floor. I'll give a reward of fifty pounds sterling silver to anyone who can get me a ladder!"

The excited throng of people surrounded the house and scurried about screaming every threat imaginable: "Break down the door...he will not get away," or "Burn the house down, we will get him then." Their voices blended together and made a mighty roar.

Inside the house, Sikes demanded, "Get me a rope. The tide is up, I'll reach the water if I let myself down through this back window, and I'll swim away."

He got through the window and was on the roof when the wrathful crowd saw him. He looked down upon them. In the eerie glow of torch lights, their faces looked like a mass of brutal eyes all staring at him with vengeance.

Quickly, Sikes looped the rope around his head and planned to put his arms through the circle to tighten it around his chest when the roar of the crowd made him look their way once more. And when he did, he thought he saw her eyes: Nancy's cold, dead eyes!

The sight made him jerk his body in terror. He lost his balance and fell over the railing. The rope, however, was still around his neck. The weight of his falling body pulled it tightly...until in an instant...he hung there dead.

CHAPTER 23

A New Family

Two days later, Oliver rode in a coach to the town where he was born. Accompanying him were Mrs. Maylie, Miss Rose, Mrs. Bedwin, and Dr. Losberne. Following them in a carriage came Mr. Brownlow and one other person.

Oliver and the ladies had been informed of most of the facts that Mr. Brownlow and Dr. Losberne had forced out of Monks, and they knew that they were on a journey to fill in the missing gaps. Still, the mystery of it all hovered over the coach and kept its occupants lost in their own thoughts.

But a flood of memories interrupted Oliver's thoughts once they left the city limits and he saw again the dusty road he had traveled all alone.

"Look, there is the house I grew up in, Miss Rose," he cried. "Do you think I will be able to see Dick?"

"Yes, dear Oliver, soon. And he will see how happy and well you are, but even happier to see him!"

"Yes, and we can take him back with us can't we? We can take care of him and make him well?" Oliver spoke through tears.

"Absolutely," Miss Rose promised.

"He blessed me, Miss Rose, before I left him on that day when I ran away," Oliver said with a smile. "Now, I can say to him, 'God bless you.'"

They drove past Sowerberry's, they drove past Gamfield's chimney sweep shop, and Oliver choked on the bad memories. But then he found the relief of understanding that those days were gone forever. And, then they drove up to the grandest hotel in the town: it had seemed like a palace to Oliver when he had walked past it as a child.

Yet, Oliver was astonished even further when they stepped out of the coach in front of the hotel and were greeted by Mr. Grimwig smiling and—not once wanting to eat his head!

Why was Mr. Grimwig here? Why are we all here? And, who was the stranger who had ridden in the carriage behind us? Oliver asked himself.

All he really knew was that they were to unpack their luggage in their rooms and then meet in the parlor. Then, however, more mystery prevailed, since Mr. Brownlow stayed in his room, which seemed most unusual. Dr. Losberne and Mr. Grimwig came in and out all the while, conversing in hushed tones. Mrs. Maylie left the parlor area for about an hour and came back with eyes red and swollen from crying. All this secret activity perplexed Oliver and Miss Rose greatly.

Then at 9 p.m., Dr. Losberne, Mr. Grimwig, and Mr. Brownlow entered the room together. They brought with them the fourth man: a stranger whose appearance startled Oliver so much that the child almost screamed.

Oliver saw before him the frightening face of the man who had bumped into him at the village post and had peeked through the window at him in the country cottage. Monks looked at the boy with hatred, then turned and took a seat at Mr. Brownlow's direction.

Mr. Brownlow rested his hand on Oliver's shoulder and said to Monks, "This young man is your half brother born to your father and a young lady named Agnes Fleming." Oliver acknowledged this remark with a look of astonishment, but said nothing.

"Yes, and he was born in the lowly pauper's workhouse in this very town," Monks spoke scornfully, "as you know, since you seem to know all the story."

"Perhaps not all, Mr. Monks. And just to be sure that I've learned all the necessary facts, I want you to tell every bit of it to us here tonight. So, begin."

Reluctantly, Monks related his history and that of his very unhappy parents. He told how he and his mother had found two documents in his father's desk after he died. One paper was a letter to Oliver's mother, Agnes, stating how much he loved her and how he hoped they would be married soon. The other document was his last will.

Mr. Brownlow here interrupted, for he had extensive knowledge of the will's content. Oliver's father had provided very generously for Monks and his mother, and also for Oliver's mother and the child she was expecting. There was, however, a special clause about the unborn child. Mr. Leeford had experienced so much hatred and rebellion from his first son (taught to the boy by his embittered mother) that he included a condition in his will. It stated that if the second child was a boy, he would receive his inheritance only if, during his youth, he did nothing to disgrace his parents.

If, however, the second son chose to live dishonorably, his inheritance would be taken from him and added to the first son's portion. Mr. Leeford had made this stipulation to help his beloved Agnes. He felt it would be hard enough to raise the child alone without her having to deal with a child like Mr. Leeford's firstborn son.

Suddenly, it became very clear to all the listeners exactly how and why Monks' selfish greed had driven him to plot the corruption of the morals of young Oliver Twist.

Monks added to Mr. Brownlow's account that before she died, his mother had destroyed that copy of the will, but had passed on to him her hatred of Agnes and the child. Monks was quite proud of how he had nurtured that hatred in his heart until it was now a consuming passion.

A few moments of shocked silence filled the room. Then Mr. Brownlow stood beside Miss Rose's chair and asked her to stand.

"My dear, there is one more matter that needs clearing up," the gentleman declared.

"Monks, it is time now that you tell us this lady's history," Mr. Brownlow directed.

Miss Rose interrupted, "What could he know of my history, kind sir? I've never seen the man before today!" Miss Rose spoke in amazement.

"He knows a great deal, my dear," Mr. Brownlow answered. "You see, Agnes had a baby sister."

Monks picked up the story, "And when Agnes' widowed father was shamed by the way she died, he moved to a faraway village just to get away from the sights and sounds of London. He never recovered from Agnes' death. When he died a short time later, a poor neighbor couple took the orphaned baby sister to their home."

"My mother," Monks continued, "discovered this arrangement. She received at least partial revenge by filling the couple's head with the poison of what a shameful woman the girl's older sister had been. My mother added to the story and said the baby girl would also come to shame herself, for it was in her blood and kin. Therefore, the couple's care and compassion of the baby began to shrink—just as my mother hoped it would! But then, a widow lady saw the child's distress and took her into her own home. Ultimately, my mother's plot failed, for Mrs. Maylie has brought you up very well...." Monks spoke defeatedly.

"Mrs. Maylie!" Miss Rose called out. "I was the baby sister? I am the sister of Oliver's poor mother!"

"Yes, dear," Mrs. Maylie replied, "as I have just learned tonight. But more importantly, please know that I love you as my own daughter and always will."

The ladies held each other as joyful tears fell down their faces. Then they opened their arms to the dear, sweet Oliver who was truly a part of the loving circle. There were so many facts for the three to absorb! Miss Rose had learned the identity of her parents and sister and now grieved their passing, but she also rejoiced at the discovery of a nephew.

Oliver had learned of his father, Edward Leeford; his mother, Agnes Fleming; an evil half brother; and a saintly aunt, Miss Rose.

Then, as yet another addition to the night's drama, Harry Maylie entered the room with the urgent purpose of talking with Miss Rose. He asked if they could see each other alone in the anteroom.

"My Rose, I could not wait any longer to see you. I learned the whole story yesterday," Harry said with lovingkindness. "Please tell me now that you feel free to be my wife. Surely, your doubts about a marriage between us are now gone."

"I wish with all my heart that they were gone. But, dear Harry, nothing has changed about what I am," Miss Rose's voice trembled.

"How do you say such a thing?" Harry disagreed.

Miss Rose explained, "Think about what we have learned: I am the daughter of a man who felt such disgrace that it killed him."

"Rose, his disgrace is not your shame," Harry reasoned. "Each of us is responsible only for the path in life we take ourselves. You, my Rose, have chosen a path filled with beauty and grace. It is a beauty and grace that I want to fill my home—my home with you—our home where we will comfort anyone who has been bruised and stained by the world just as you and sweet Agnes were."

"How can this be, dear Harry?" asked Miss Rose.

"It has happened as a result of our last conversation, sweet Rose, where my heart was broken as you reminded me of my vain and

empty goals. You painted a picture for me of my future that contained great position, fame, and fortune, but which broke my heart because there was no room for love."

Harry continued, "Your words have influenced me all these months that we have been apart, and I have used their influence to change my ways for the better. Dear Rose, I have entered the seminary to train for the ministry. The home I wish to open to you will be a clergyman's home where you and I, together, can serve the needs of broken souls and bring God's love to all His children."

A sweet expression of delight came over Rose's face. She placed her hand in the hand of her beloved, and they walked back to the parlor.

As you can imagine, dear reader, the evening's long discussion of weighty matters had delayed supper way past its usual time.

Mr. Grimwig, who had fallen asleep in his parlor chair while Miss Rose and Mr. Maylie were in the anteroom, was awakened with growling hunger pains.

He opened his eyes to see everyone appearing nearly as starved as he was. At that moment, Harry and Miss Rose re-entered the parlor, arm in arm.

"Shall we retire to the dining room where we may eat and drink a toast to the future bride and groom, I presume?" Mr. Grimwig said cheerfully.

All faces turned toward the handsome couple as the two lovers blushed with happiness.

"Good! It is about time these matters were all settled," Mr. Grimwig announced, "for I am so hungry I'm about to eat my head!"

CHAPTER 24

To Each His Own Reward

Several days later, the largest courtroom in London could not contain all the angry people who wanted a look at the wretched man named Fagin. They wanted to jeer him for corrupting so many youths, even bringing one of them to a cruel and untimely death. They wanted to hear the verdict and see justice work.

The mob had nearly scratched his eyes out as the police had dragged him to court that day. He was unshaven, and perspiration and blood had matted down his red hair and beard.

The courtroom was hot and stifling. As Fagin awaited the jury's decision, he tried to think of anything and everything except the death sentence that he knew was coming.

Soon, the jury returned to their seats with the decision.

A wave of silence came over everyone in the packed gallery spaces. No one spoke, no one moved. All eyes, including Fagin's, followed the jury master as he cleared his throat, opened his lips, and said, simply, "Guilty."

The crowd roared with approval. Their unanimous voices sounded like thunder. They all knew the hanging would be on Monday.

The only silent person in the entire hall was Fagin himself, who sat hunched over in his chair looking at his feet.

Then the jailer led Fagin to a solitary jail cell where his thoughts finally considered the words he had just heard from the judge: Death by hanging.

In the cold, dark cell, Fagin suddenly thought of all the other criminals he had seen hanged in his own lifetime—many of them for crimes Fagin had taught them to commit. He even remembered laughing at some of them for praying for mercy as they were led to the gallows. Now, he was in the same final cell. His evil conscience tortured his soul in ways perhaps more deadly than would the hangman's rope.

Fagin spent several days in prison, but never once repented of his deeds. When, at last on Monday morning, the gallows' attendants came to take him away, they found him trembling and muttering disjointed words as if he had lost his mind.

Oliver and Mr. Brownlow were in the crowd of witnesses to the execution that day. It was a terrifying end.

Three months later, Miss Rose Fleming and Mr. Harry Maylie were married in the village church where he had just been called as minister. They made their home in the neat and pretty parsonage. Mrs. Maylie also moved in and happily joined the family circle.

Dr. Losberne rented a country cottage close enough to the village church so that he could attend services every Sunday. He and Mr. Grimwig became very good friends and found it great fun to discuss Mr. Maylie's sermons every Sunday afternoon.

Mr. Grimwig also seldom failed to recall to his other friend, Mr. Brownlow, how they had sat that night many months before waiting for Oliver's return. Mr. Grimwig commented often how he had been right after all, for Oliver did not return that night! At this remembrance, everyone would always have a good laugh!

Charley Bates was brought to his senses by the cruel death of his friend, Nancy, and the horrific end of Sikes and Fagin. Charley learned the trade of cattle ranching and lived an honest, contented, country life thereafter.

The workhouse supervisor learned of the underhanded connection the Bumbles had had with Monks and how Mrs. Bumble had taken advantage of Miss Sally's trust. For their dishonesty, Mr. and Mrs. Bumble were removed from their positions of official and workhouse maid. Having no other way to make a living, they became paupers themselves.

Monks took his part of his father's inheritance and traveled far away. Although he could have used the second chance to start his life over afresh, he lived in the same dishonest ways and died in prison.

Mr. Brownlow adopted Oliver to raise him as his own dear son. He passed on to Oliver all his accumulated knowledge and shared with him all the good memories he had of his friend, Edward Leeford. Since Mr. Brownlow had never had a family of his own, and since Oliver needed the nurturing of one who had known his father so well, it was a mutually satisfying and happy life. The only mark of pain came on the day that Oliver learned that his little friend, Dick, had died.

Oliver thinks of Dick often as he sits in the garden outside the village church. There, surrounded by a beautiful bed of yellow roses, is a memorial plaque engraved with the name, Agnes. Oliver remembers the blessing of his little friend, Dick, and the dying love of his own dear mother, and he is comforted to see the remembrance there. He believes it is fitting that her memorial should be found in a church's garden; for though she was weak and erring, surely she has found the mercy of the Lord.